Sunlight and Shadows

A Josefina Classic
Volume 1

by Valerie Tripp

★ American Girl®

Published by American Girl Publishing
Copyright © 1997, 2000, 2014 American Girl

Questions or comments? Call 1-800-845-0005,
visit **americangirl.com**, or write to Customer Service,
American Girl, 8400 Fairway Place, Middleton, WI 53562.

Printed in China
15 16 17 18 19 20 21 LEO 12 11 10 9 8 7 6 5 4

All American Girl marks, BeForever™, Josefina®,
and Josefina Montoya® are trademarks of American Girl.

Grateful acknowledgment is made to the following for permission
to quote previously published material: p. 99—Enrique R. Lamadrid
(excerpt from "Las mañanitas/Little morning song" in *Tesoros del espíritu:
A portrait in sound of Hispanic New Mexico*, University of New Mexico Press,
© 1994 Enrique R. Lamadrid); p. 112—University of Oklahoma Press
(verse published in *The Folklore of Spain in the American Southwest*, by
Aurelio M. Espinosa, edited by J. Manuel Espinosa, © 1985 University
of Oklahoma Press, Norman, Publishing Division of the University).

Grateful acknowledgment is made to María C De Baca, Las Vegas, NM, for
permission to quote the verses appearing on pp. 154, 156, 167, 168, and 169,
originally published in the booklet *The Christmas Season* by Elba C De Baca.

Cover image by Michael Dwornik and Juliana Kolesova

Library of Congress Cataloging-in-Publication Data
Tripp, Valerie, 1951–
Sunlight and shadows : a Josefina classic. volume 1 / Valerie Tripp.
pages   cm — (BeForever)
Summary: Josefina and her sisters are excited when energetic young Aunt
Dolores arrives at the rancho, bringing new ideas, new fashions, and new
challenges, but they worry the changes will make them forget Mamá, especially
as Christmas approaches.
ISBN 978-1-60958-552-5 (paperback) — ISBN 978-1-60958-553-2 (ebook)
[1. Ranch life—New Mexico—Fiction. 2. Sisters—Fiction. 3. Aunts—Fiction.
4. Mexican Americans—Fiction. 5. New Mexico—History—To 1848—Fiction.]
I. Title.
PZ7.T7363Sun 2014   [Fic]—dc23   2014022873

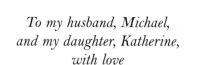

To my husband, Michael,
and my daughter, Katherine,
with love

To my mother,
Kathleen Martin Tripp,
with love

To Granger William Tripp
and Paige Elizabeth Tripp,
with love

Beforever

The adventurous characters you'll meet in
the BeForever books will spark your curiosity
about the past, inspire you to find your voice
in the present, and excite you about your future.
You'll make friends with these girls as you share
their fun and their challenges. Like you, they are
bright and brave, imaginative and energetic,
creative and kind. Just as you are, they are
discovering what really matters: Helping others.
Being a true friend. Protecting the earth.
Standing up for what's right. Read their stories,
explore their worlds, join their adventures.
Your friendship with them will BeForever.

TABLE *of* CONTENTS

Josefina and her family speak Spanish, so you'll
see some Spanish words in this book. You'll find
the meanings and pronunciations of these words
in the glossary on page 174.

Remember that in Spanish, "j" is pronounced
like "h." That means Josefina's name is
pronounced "ho-seh-FEE-nah."

Primroses

Josefina Montoya hummed to herself as she stood in the sunshine waiting for her three sisters. It was a bright, breezy morning in late summer and the girls were going to the stream to wash clothes. Josefina's basket was full of laundry to be washed, but she didn't mind. She enjoyed going to the stream on a day like this. The sky was a deep, strong blue. Josefina wished she could touch it. She was sure it would feel smooth and cool.

Josefina liked to stand just in front of her house, where the life of her papá's *rancho* was going on all around her. From here, she could smell the sharp scent of smoke from the kitchen fire. She could see cows and sheep grazing in the pastures. Yellow grass rolled all the way to the dark green trees on the foothills of the mountains, and the mountains zigzagged up to the sky.

She could hear all the sounds of the rancho: chickens clucking, donkeys braying, dogs barking, birds chirping, workers hammering, and someone laughing. The sounds seemed like music to Josefina. The wind joined in the music when it rustled the leaves on the cottonwood trees. And always, under it all, was the murmur of the stream.

Josefina shaded her eyes. Even from this far away, she could see Papá. He sat very straight and tall on his horse. He was talking to the workers in the cornfield near the stream. The rancho had belonged to Papá's family for more than one hundred years. All those years, Papá's family had cared for the animals and the land. It was not an easy life. Everyone had to work hard. Some years there was plenty of rain so that the crops grew and the animals were healthy. Some years there was not enough rain. Then the soil was dry and the animals went thirsty. But through good times and bad the rancho went on. It provided everything Josefina and her family needed to live. It gave them food, clothing, and shelter. Josefina loved the rancho. It had been her home all the nine years of her life. She believed that it was the most beautiful place in all of New Mexico and all of the world.

Josefina was dancing a little dance of impatience
to go with the song she was humming when her oldest
sister, Ana, came outside to join her.

"Josefina," Ana said. "You remind me of a little
bird, singing and hopping from one foot to the other
like that."

"If I were a bird," said Josefina with a grin, "I could
have flown to the stream and back twenty times by
now. I've been waiting and waiting for you! Where are
Francisca and Clara?"

Ana sighed. "They're coming," she said. "They
couldn't agree on whose turn it was to carry the washing tub."

Josefina and Ana looked at each other and shook
their heads. They were the eldest and youngest of
the four sisters, and they got along beautifully. But
Francisca and Clara, the middle sisters, often dis-
agreed. It was always over some silly little thing. They
reminded Josefina of goats she had seen ramming into
each other head-to-head for no particular reason.

When the girls appeared at last, it was easy to
see who had won the argument. Francisca, looking

pleased with herself, carried only a basket of laundry balanced on her head. Clara, looking cross, carried the large copper washing tub.

Josefina put her basket into the copper tub. "I'll take one handle of the tub, Clara," she said. "We'll carry it between us."

Clara said, "*Gracias.*" But she sounded more grumpy than grateful.

Josefina knew a way to cheer her up. "Let's race to the stream!" she said.

"Oh, no . . ." Francisca began to say. She didn't like to do anything that might muss her clothes or her hair.

But Josefina and Clara had already taken off running, so Ana and Francisca had to run, too.

The sisters flew down the dirt path that sloped past the fruit trees, past the fields, and to the stream. Josefina and Clara reached the stream first, plunked the tub down, kicked off their moccasins, and ran into the shallow water. Then they turned and scooped up handfuls of water to splash Ana and Francisca, who shrieked with laughter as the water hit them.

"Stop!" cried Francisca. She held up her basket to shield her face.

"Now, girls," Ana scolded gently. "We've come to wash the clothes that are in our baskets, *not* the ones we're wearing!"

Josefina and Clara stopped splashing. They were out of breath anyway. They filled the copper tub with water from the stream. Josefina knelt next to the tub. She took the root of a yucca plant out of the little leather pouch she wore at her waist and then pounded it between two rocks. The shredded yucca root made a nice lather of soapy bubbles in the water. Josefina put a dirty shirt in the tub and scrubbed it all over. Then she swooshed it around in the stream to rinse out the soap.

The sun was hot on her head and her back, and the water was cool on her arms and hands. Josefina liked to think about how the water started out as snow on the mountaintops. It melted and flowed all the way down to this little pool in the stream without ever losing its cool freshness. She knew that it was water that brought life to the rancho. Water from the stream was channeled into ditches so that it would flow through the fields. Without water, nothing would grow.

Josefina twisted the shirt to wring it out, and watched drops of water fall back into the stream and go on their way. Then she carefully spread the shirt on top of a bush.

"The sun and the breeze will dry the clothes quickly today," she said as she washed some socks.

"Yes," agreed Ana. "Mamá would have said, 'You see, girls? God has sent us a good drying day. Monday is laundry day even in heaven.'"

"And then Mamá would have said, 'Pull your *rebozos* up to shade your faces, girls. You don't want your skin to look like old leather!'" added Francisca as she adjusted her shawl on her head. Francisca was always careful of her skin.

The sisters laughed softly together and then grew quiet. Speaking of their mamá always made them thoughtful. Mamá had died the year before. The sorrow of her death was always in their hearts.

Josefina looked at the stream flowing past and listened to its low, rushing sound. Since Mamá died she had learned a truth that was both bitter and sweet. She had learned that love does not end. Josefina would always love Mamá, and so she would always miss her.

Josefina knew her sisters were also thinking about Mamá because Francisca said, "Look. See those yellow flowers across the stream?" She pointed with a soapy hand. "Aren't they evening primroses? They're in the shade, so they haven't wilted yet this morning. Mamá used to love those flowers."

"Yes, she did," said Clara, agreeing with Francisca for once. "Why don't you pick some, Josefina? You could dry them and put them in your memory box."

"All right," said Josefina. Papá had given her a little wooden box of Mamá's. Josefina called it her memory box because in it she kept small things that reminded her of Mamá, such as a piece of Mamá's favorite lavender-scented soap. The box had been made by Josefina's great-great-grandfather. On its top there was a carving of the sun coming up over the highest mountain and shining on the rancho just the way Josefina saw it rise every morning.

The quickest, driest way to the primroses was to walk across a fallen log that made a narrow bridge over the stream. Josefina climbed up onto the log. She held her arms out for balance and began to walk across.

"Oh, do be careful," warned Ana. Because she was

the oldest sister, Ana had become a motherly worrier
since Mamá died.

Josefina did not think of herself as a brave person
at all. She was afraid of snakes and lightning and guns,
and shy of people she didn't know. But she wasn't
afraid of crossing the log, which wasn't very high
above the stream anyway. She walked across, picked
the primroses, and tucked the stems in her pouch. She
let the yellow flowers stick out so that they wouldn't
be crushed. On the way back, she decided to tease Ana
to make her laugh. She pretended to lose her balance.
She waved her arms wildly up and down and wobbled
more and more with each step.

"Josefina Montoya!" said Ana, who saw that she
was fooling. "How can you be so shy and sweet in
company when you're so playful with your sisters?
You tease the life out of me. You'll make me old before
my time!"

"You sound just like our grandfather," said Josefina
as she jumped to the ground.

She pretended to talk like Abuelito. "Yes, yes, yes,
my beautiful granddaughters! This was the finest trip
I've ever made! Oh, the adventures, the adventures!

But this was my last trip. Oh, how these trips age me!
They make me—"

"—old before my time!" all the sisters sang out
together. Abuelito said the same thing after every
journey.

Abuelito was their mamá's father. He was a trader,
and once each year he organized a huge caravan. The
caravan was made up of many carts pulled by oxen and
many mules carrying packs. The carts and the mules
were loaded with wool, hides, and blankets in New
Mexico. Then the caravan traveled more than a thou-
sand miles south to Mexico City. The trail the caravans
used was called the *Camino Real*.

When Abuelito got to Mexico City, he traded the
goods he'd brought from New Mexico for things from
all over the world. He traded for silk and cotton goods
and lace, for iron tools, paper, ink, books, fine dishes,
coffee, and sugar. Then the caravan would load up and
start the long trip back to New Mexico.

Abuelito had been gone more than six months.
Josefina and her sisters were excited because they
expected Abuelito's caravan to return any day now.
Their rancho was always the caravan's last stop before

the town of Santa Fe, where Abuelito lived.

"I can't wait until Abuelito comes!" said Josefina. She thought that the arrival of the caravan was the most exciting thing that happened on the rancho. The wagons were full of treasures to be traded in Santa Fe. But the most important treasure the caravan brought was Abuelito himself, safe and sound and full of wonderful stories. Sometimes the caravan went through sandstorms that were so bad they blocked out the sun. Sometimes robbers or wild animals attacked the caravan. Sometimes the caravan had to cross flooded rivers or waterless deserts. Abuelito loved to tell about his adventures, and the sisters loved to listen.

"I am going to go on the caravan with Abuelito someday," said Francisca, dreamily swirling a shirt in the stream. "I'll see everything there is to see, and then I'll settle down and live in Mexico City with Mamá's sister, our Tía Dolores. I am sure she lives in a grand house and knows all the most elegant people."

Clara rolled her eyes and scrubbed hard with her soap. "That's ridiculous," she said. "We hardly know Tía Dolores. We haven't seen her for the whole ten years she's been living in Mexico City."

Francisca smiled a superior smile. "I am older than you are, Clara," she said. "I was nearly six when Tía Dolores left. I remember her."

"Well," said Clara tartly. "If *she* remembers *you,* I am sure she won't want you to live with her!"

Francisca made a face and was about to say something sharp when Josefina piped up.

"Ana," said Josefina, trying to keep the peace. "What do you hope Abuelito will bring on the caravan?"

"Shoes for Juan and Antonio," Ana answered. She and her husband, Tomás, had two little boys—Josefina's beloved nephews.

"I hope he brings that plow Papá needs," said Clara. She was always practical.

"How dull!" said Francisca. "*I'm* hoping for some new lace."

"You think too much of how you look," said Clara.

Francisca smirked. "Perhaps you ought—" she began.

But Josefina interrupted again. "Well, I know one thing we *all* hope Abuelito will bring," she said cheerfully. "Chocolate!"

"Lots!" said Francisca and Clara. They spoke at exactly the same moment, which made them laugh at each other.

"You haven't said what you're wishing for," Ana said to Josefina. She was squeezing water out of a petticoat. "Perhaps you're hoping for a surprise."

"Perhaps," said Josefina, smiling.

The truth was, she didn't know how to name what she wished for. What she wanted most was for her sisters to be at peace with one another. She wanted the household to be running smoothly, and Papá to be happy and laughing and making music again. She longed for life to be the way it was when Mamá was alive.

Right after Mamá died, Josefina had felt that the world should end. How could life go on for the rest of them without Mamá? It had seemed wrong, even cruel somehow, that nothing stopped. The sun rose and set. Seasons passed from one to another. There were still chores to be done every day. There were clothes to be washed, weeds to pull, animals to be fed, socks to be mended.

But as time went by, Josefina began to see that the

steady rhythm of life on the rancho was her best comfort. Mamá seemed close by when Josefina and her
sisters were together doing the laundry or mending or
cooking or cleaning. The sisters tried hard to do the
chores the way that Mamá had taught them. Every day,
they tried to remember their prayers and their manners
and how to do things right. But it was not easy without
Mamá's loving guidance.

Josefina looked at the primroses in her pouch and
thought of Mamá. Mamá had such faith in them all!
She brought out the best in them. Now that she was
gone, they struggled. Francisca and Clara squabbled.
Ana worried. Josefina often felt lost and unsure. And
Papá was very quiet. He had given his violin away, so
he never filled the house with music anymore. Josefina
sighed. She didn't see how the caravan could bring
anything to help them.

"Here comes a surprise," said Clara. "But not one
you will like, Josefina."

Josefina looked up. "Oh, no," she said.

It was a small herd of goats. They were coming
down the hill to drink from the stream. Josefina disliked all goats and one goat in particular. The biggest,

oldest, meanest goat was named Florecita. Florecita was a sneaky, nasty bully. She bit, she rammed, and she'd eat anything. Josefina was afraid of her. She frowned when she spotted Florecita at the edge of the herd.

"Now, Josefina," said Ana when she saw her frowning. "You mustn't dislike *these* goats. This is *our* herd."

Most of the rancho's sheep and goats were still in the summer pastures up in the mountains. But this herd was kept close to the rancho to provide milk to drink and to make into cheese. It was a small herd that had belonged to Mamá. She left the herd to Josefina and her sisters when she died. Josefina wished she hadn't. Mamá had always protected Josefina from things she feared and disliked, and Mamá had protected Josefina from the goats. "The goats are everything you are not, Josefina," Mamá used to say. "They are bold and loud and disagreeable and mean. It's no wonder you dislike them!" Josefina was sure that Mamá never intended her to have anything to do with the goats, so she avoided them as much as possible.

But right now, Josefina saw Florecita headed straight for her.

"She wants the flowers in your pouch!" warned Francisca.

Josefina put one hand over the flowers. She did not want Florecita to have them. They might be the last primroses of the year!

"Shoo!" she said to Florecita feebly, waving her free hand. "Go away!"

"Shoo! Shoo! Shoo!" cried her sisters with more force.

Florecita didn't even slow down. She kept walking steadily toward Josefina. Her yellow eyes were fixed on the primroses in Josefina's pouch.

"Wave a stick at her," suggested Francisca.

"Splash her," suggested Ana.

"Throw a pebble at her," suggested Clara.

But Josefina backed away. She had been poked by Florecita's sharp horns before, and she had no wish to be poked again. She scrambled up and stood on the log over the stream. Still Florecita did not stop coming. Josefina took one backward step, then another, then *SPLASH!* She missed her footing and fell off the log into the stream. It was very shallow, so she landed hard on the bottom.

"Oh, no!" she wailed. She saw that all but one sprig of the primroses had fallen out of her pouch. The flowers were floating on the water. Florecita snatched them up in her mean-looking teeth. She chewed them, looking satisfied. Then the goat turned and sauntered off to rejoin the herd.

"Are you all right?" Ana asked kindly. She helped Josefina to her feet. "You really must not let Florecita bully you like that!"

Josefina wrung out her skirt and smiled. "I tried to stand up to Florecita," she joked, "but I ended up sitting down, didn't I?"

She laughed along with her sisters, but she was annoyed with Florecita. She was even more annoyed with herself for letting Florecita scare her. As she looked at the one sprig of primroses left in her pouch, she thought of another thing she wanted that the caravan could not possibly bring her—the courage to stand up to Florecita!

Abuelito's Surprise

The afternoon sun was so strong it made the ground shimmer. Josefina dipped the drinking gourd into the water jar and took a long drink. Like everyone else on the rancho, she was up earlier than usual after her *siesta*, the mid-day rest. Papá had heard that the caravan was not far away. It would come this afternoon! Everyone was eagerly bustling about, preparing for its arrival.

Josefina poured some water into her cupped hand and held it to her face, cooling first one cheek and then the other. Then she opened her hand and let the water fall on a small cluster of flowers below. Mamá had planted these flowers, which grew in a protected corner of the back courtyard. Josefina's house was built around two square courtyards. The front courtyard was surrounded by rooms where Josefina and her family lived. The back courtyard was surrounded by workrooms, storerooms, and rooms for the servants. The two courtyards were connected by a narrow passageway.

Mamá, with Josefina at her side, had tended her flowers in the back courtyard with great devotion. She started them from seeds sent to her from Mexico City by her sister, Tía Dolores. Josefina remembered how pleased Mamá had always been when the caravan brought her some seeds from Tía Dolores. It had always seemed like a miracle to Josefina that the small brown seeds could, with water and Mamá's care, grow into beautiful, colorful flowers. Since Mamá died, Josefina had cared for the flowers by herself as best she could. Just now she sprinkled the rest of the water in the drinking gourd on them.

"I'm glad you remember to water your mamá's flowers, Josefina." Josefina turned and saw Papá. He was so tall, she had to lift her chin to look at his face. "Things grew well for your mamá, didn't they?" Papá added.

"Yes, Papá," Josefina answered. "Mamá loved her flowers."

"So she did," said Papá, dipping the drinking gourd into the water jar. "And I hear Florecita likes flowers, too."

Josefina blushed.

"Don't worry," said Papá. "You'll stand up to Florecita when you're ready."

Josefina grinned a little bashfully. She watched Papá drink his water. Papá's eyebrows were so thick, he looked fierce until you saw the kindness in his eyes. All the sisters were respectful and rather shy of Papá. He had always been saving of his words, but since Mamá died he'd become especially quiet. Josefina knew his silence didn't come from sternness or anger. It came from sadness. She knew because she often felt the same way.

Mamá used to say that Josefina and Papá were alike. They were both quiet, except with their family, but full of ideas inside! Papá didn't have Mamá's easy manner with people. It had always been Mamá who remembered the names of everyone in the village, from the oldest person to the newest baby. She remembered to ask if an illness was better, or how the chickens were laying. She gave advice on everything from growing squash to dyeing wool. Mamá was well loved and well respected. She was Papá's partner. She ran the household while he ran the rancho. Josefina knew that Papá missed Mamá with all his heart.

Papá tipped the gourd so that the last drops of water fell on the flowers. He smiled at Josefina, and then strode off out the gate toward the fields.

Josefina carried the water jar to the kitchen.

"Oh, there you are, Josefina," said Ana. Her hands were covered with flour, so she had to use the back of her wrist to brush the sweat off her forehead. The heat of the cooking fires was making her face red and her hair stick out. Pots full of delicious-smelling concoctions sizzled, steamed, and burbled over the fires.

There was always a big party with music and dancing, called a *fandango,* in the evening after the caravan arrived. Neighbors from the little town nearby, friends from the Indian *pueblo* village, and all the people traveling with the caravan were invited. They came to Josefina's family's house to eat and drink and sing and dance and celebrate the caravan's safe return. Mamá had always known just what to do to prepare for the fandango. But this was the first time Ana was in charge. Josefina could see that Ana was overwhelmed even though Carmen, the cook, was helping her. Two other servants were making *tortillas* as quickly as they could. Francisca and Clara were helping, too. They were peeling, chopping, and stirring as fast as their hands could move.

"Thank you for the water," said Ana. She handed Josefina a large basket. "Now please go to the kitchen garden and get me some onions."

"I'll come, too," Francisca said. "We need tomatoes."

The kitchen garden was just outside the back courtyard. Josefina always thought the garden looked like a blanket spread on the ground. The neat rows of fruits and vegetables and herbs made colorful stripes. The squash made a yellow stripe. The chiles made a red stripe. The pumpkins were orange, the melons were light green, and the beans were dark green. In between the rows, the earth was a dark reddish-brown, thanks to the water the girls carried up from the stream every day. A stick fence like a blanket's fringe surrounded the garden to keep hungry animals out. The sisters were all proud of the garden.

Josefina had gathered a basketful of onions when

suddenly she stood up. Francisca stood up, too, and the girls looked at each other.

"Is it . . . ?" Francisca began.

"Shhh . . ." said Josefina, holding her finger to her lips. She tilted her head and listened hard. Yes! There it was. She could hear the rumble and squeak of wooden wheels that meant only one thing. The caravan was coming!

Francisca heard, too. The girls smiled at each other, grabbed their baskets, and ran as fast as they could back through the gate. "The caravan! It's coming!" they shouted. "Ana! Clara! It's coming!" They dropped their baskets outside the kitchen door as Clara rushed out to join them.

The three girls dashed across the front courtyard and flew up the steps of the tower in the south wall. The window in the tower was narrow, so Josefina knelt and looked out the lower part. Francisca and Clara stood behind her and looked over her head.

At first, all they saw was a cloud of dust stirring on the road from the village. Then the sound of the wheels grew louder and louder. Soon they heard the jingle of harnesses, dogs barking, people shouting,

and the village church bell ringing. Next they saw
soldiers coming over the hill with the sun glinting on
their buttons and guns. Then came mule after mule. It
looked like a hundred or more to Josefina. The mules
were carrying heavy packs strapped to their backs.
She counted thirty carts pulled by plodding oxen.
The carts lumbered along on their two big wooden
wheels. There were four-wheeled wagons as well. And
so many people! Too many to count! There were cart
drivers, traders, and whole families of travelers. There
were herders driving sheep, goats, and cattle. People
from town and Indians from the nearby pueblo village
walked along with the caravan to welcome it.

Francisca stood on tiptoe to see better. She put
her hands on Josefina's shoulders. "Don't you love to
think about all the places the caravan has been?" she
asked. "And all the places the things it brings come
from, too?"

"Yes," said Josefina. "They come from all over the
world, up the Camino Real, right to *our* door!"

Most of the caravan stopped and set up camp mid-
way between the town and the rancho. But many of the
cart drivers camped closer to the house, in a shady area

next to the stream. Josefina saw Papá ride his horse up to one of the big, four-wheeled wagons. He waved to its driver.

"That's Abuelito!" Josefina cried. She pointed to the driver of the four-wheeled wagon. "Look! Papá is greeting him. See? There he is!"

Francisca leaned forward. "Who's that tall woman sitting next to Abuelito?" she wondered aloud. "She's greeting Papá as if she knows him."

But Josefina and Clara had already turned away from the window. They hurried down from the tower. Josefina ran to the kitchen and stuck her head in the door. "Come on," she said to Ana. "Papá and Abuelito are on their way up to the house."

"Oh dear, oh dear," fussed Ana as she wiped her hands and smoothed her hair. "There's still so much to do. I'll never be ready for the fandango."

When Papá led Abuelito's big wagon up to the front gate, Josefina was the first to run out and greet it. Francisca, Clara, and Ana were close behind. Josefina thought she'd never seen a sight as wonderful as Abuelito's happy face. He handed the reins to the woman next to him and climbed down.

"My beautiful granddaughters!" said Abuelito. He kissed them as he named them. "Ana, and Francisca! Clara, and my little Josefina! Oh, God bless you! God bless you! It is good to see you! This was the finest trip I've ever made! Oh, the adventures, the adventures! But I am getting too old for these trips. They make me old before my time. This is my last trip. My last."

"Oh, Abuelito!" said Francisca, taking his arm and laughing. "You say that every time!"

Abuelito threw back his head and laughed, too. "Ah, but this time I mean it," he said. "I've brought a surprise for you." He turned and held out his hand to the tall woman on the wagon. "Here she is, your Tía Dolores. She has come back to live with her mamá and me in Santa Fe. Now I have no reason to go to Mexico City ever again!"

Josefina and her sisters looked so surprised, Papá and Abuelito laughed at them. Tía Dolores took Abuelito's hand and gracefully swung herself down from the wagon seat.

Papá smiled at her. "You see, Dolores? You have surprised my daughters as much as you surprised me," he said. "Welcome to our home."

"Gracias," Tía Dolores answered. She smiled at Papá and then she turned to the sisters. "I've looked forward to this moment for a long time!" she said to them. "I've wanted to see all of you! My dear sister's children!"

She spoke to each one in turn. "You're very like your mamá, Ana," she said. "And Francisca, you've grown so tall and so beautiful! Dear Clara, you were barely three years old when I left. Do you remember?"

Tía Dolores took Josefina's hand in both of her own. She bent forward so that she could look closely at Josefina's face. "At last I meet you, Josefina," she said. "You weren't even born when I left. And look! Here you are! Already a lovely young girl!" Tía Dolores straightened again. Her eyes were bright as she looked at all the sisters. "I'm so happy to see you all. It's good to be back."

The girls were still too surprised to say much, but they smiled shyly at Tía Dolores. Ana was the first to collect herself. "Please, Abuelito and Tía Dolores. Come inside and have a cool drink. I'm sure you're tired and thirsty." She led Tía Dolores inside the gate. "You must excuse us, Tía Dolores," she said. "We haven't prepared any place for you to sleep."

"Goodness, Ana!" said Tía Dolores. "You didn't know I was coming. I didn't know myself, really, until the last minute. I've been caring for my dear aunt in Mexico City all these years. Bless her soul! She died this past spring. It was just before Abuelito's caravan arrived. I had no reason to stay. So, I joined the caravan to come home."

"Yes," Abuelito said to the girls. "Your grandmother will be so pleased! Wait till Dolores and I get to Santa Fe the day after tomorrow! What a surprise, eh?"

Josefina could not take her eyes off Tía Dolores as everyone sat down together in the family *sala*. The room's thick walls and small windows kept it cool even in the heat of the afternoon.

Francisca whispered, "Isn't Tía Dolores's dress beautiful? Her sleeves must be the latest style from Europe."

But Josefina hadn't noticed Tía Dolores's sleeves, or anything else about her clothes. *This is Tía Dolores*, she kept thinking. *This is Mamá's sister.*

Josefina studied Tía Dolores to see if she looked like Mamá. Mamá had been the older of the two sisters, but Tía Dolores was much taller. She didn't have Mamá's soft, rounded beauty, Josefina decided, nor her pale skin or dark, smooth hair. Everything about Tía Dolores was sharper somehow. Her hands were bigger. Her face was more narrow. She had gray eyes and dark red hair that was springy. Her voice didn't sound like Mamá's, either. Mamá's voice was high and breathy, like notes from a flute. Tía Dolores's voice had a graceful sound. It was as low and clear as notes from a harp string. But when Tía Dolores laughed, Josefina was startled. Her laugh sounded so much like Mamá's! If Josefina closed her eyes, it might be Mamá laughing.

There was a great deal of laughter in the family sala that afternoon as Abuelito told the story of his trip. Josefina sat next to Abuelito, her arms wrapped around her knees. She was happy. It reminded her of the old days to sit with her family this way and listen to Abuelito tell about his adventures.

"This was the most remarkable trip I've ever had," said Abuelito. "Oh, the trip to Mexico City was dull enough. But on the way home! Bless my soul! What an adventure! We were in terrible danger. Terrible! Terrible! And your Tía Dolores saved us."

"Oh, but I didn't—" Tía Dolores began.

"No, no, no, my dear daughter! You *did* save us,"

said Abuelito. He turned to Papá and the girls. "You
see," he said, "I was so glad that Dolores was going
to come home with me. I finished all my business
in Mexico City as quickly as I could. All went well
until the day I came to Dolores's house to load up her
belongings. Then the trouble began." He lowered his
voice, pretending he did not want Tía Dolores to hear.
"I had forgotten how stubborn your Tía Dolores is.
She is perhaps the most stubborn woman in the world.
What did she insist that we bring? You'll never guess!
Her piano!"

Amazed, the girls all repeated, "Her *piano*?"

"Yes!" said Abuelito. He was pleased to have aston-
ished them all. "Such fuss and trouble! I told her it was
too heavy and too big! But she said she'd sooner leave
all her other belongings than her piano. So I grumbled,
but I allowed the piano to be packed and loaded onto
one of my wagons. We left Mexico City, and I complained about the piano every mile of the way." He
shook his head. "Your Tía Dolores never said a word.
She just let me go on and on, complaining. Well, then
we came to Dead Man's Canyon. And do you know
what happened?"

"What?" asked the girls.

"Thieves!" cried Abuelito in a voice so loud the girls jumped. "Thieves attacked the caravan! Oh, you've never seen such a fight! Shouting, swordfights, gunshots! The wagon with the piano was just behind ours. We saw two thieves climb up on it and push the driver onto the ground. Then six or seven of our men rushed over and wrestled with the two thieves, trying to pull them off the wagon. With all the yelling and fighting, the oxen harnessed to that wagon were scared. They bumbled into each other trying to get away. The wagon lurched forward, right to the edge of a deep gully. And then *crash*! Over it fell! Into the gully!"

The girls gasped.

Abuelito put his hand on his heart. "God bless us and save us all! What a sound that piano made when it fell!" he said. "A thud, and then a hollow *BOOM* that rumbled like musical thunder! It sounded like a giant had strummed all the keys in one stroke. The terrible sound bounced off the walls of Dead Man's Canyon. It seemed to grow louder with every echo. The thieves were terrified! They'd never heard such a sound in all their lives. Well! Didn't they take off as if they were on fire? All of them ran away as fast as their thieving legs could carry them! I'll bet they are still running!"

Everyone laughed. Abuelito laughed most of all, remembering with pleasure how frightened the thieves were. When he stopped laughing he said, "After that, I put the piano in my own wagon. I never complained again. And so you see! Dolores did save us all, by insisting that we bring her piano."

"Well done, Dolores!" said Papá.

"But Abuelito," said Josefina. "Was the piano badly hurt?"

Tía Dolores answered. "No, child," she said. "One leg is splintered, and the top is scratched. But I think it will sound fine."

"Oh," Josefina blurted, "may we see it?"

"No, no, no," said Abuelito. "We had to rebuild the crate. It's too much trouble to open it up. You'll just have to come to Santa Fe sometime to hear your aunt play."

Papá cleared his throat. "The girls and I have never seen or heard a piano," he said. "May I open the crate? I'll close it up afterward."

Tía Dolores turned to Abuelito. "Please," she said. "I'd like the girls to hear the piano."

Abuelito laughed and shrugged. "Of course, my dear, of course!" he said. "How can I say no to you after you saved my caravan?"

Tía Dolores kissed him. Then she and Papá led the girls outside to the wagon. The piano was in a big wooden crate. Papá pried a few boards off the crate. Tía Dolores climbed into the wagon. She reached into the crate and pushed back the lid that protected the piano's keys. She couldn't stand up straight, and she didn't have much room to move her hands, but she played a chord. And then, as Papá and the four girls listened, she played a spirited tune.

Josefina felt the music thrum through her whole body. It made her shiver with delight. The notes were muffled because the piano was in the wooden crate, but to Josefina, the notes sounded as beautiful as bells all chiming together in harmony. She had never heard music like the piano's music before. The notes were so full, so perfect and delicate, that Josefina imagined she could almost see them as they filled the air.

Josefina listened. She realized that, through the

music, Tía Dolores was telling them how happy she was. The music expressed her happiness better than words ever could, because it made all of them hearing it happy, too. Josefina stood still, barely breathing, listening hard until Tía Dolores stopped.

"Oh, dear," said Tía Dolores. "I'm afraid the piano's a little out of tune and I'm a little out of practice." Gently, she closed the lid over the keys.

Josefina wanted very much to touch the piano keys. She wanted to make the wonderful music happen herself. But she was too shy to ask Tía Dolores, so she said nothing.

"Gracias, Dolores," said Papá as he helped her climb down from the wagon.

"Oh, yes, gracias," said Ana, Francisca, and Clara.

"You must all come to see me in Santa Fe," said Tía Dolores, smiling. "I'll play for you, and show you how to play the piano yourselves."

The three oldest sisters followed Tía Dolores back inside the house. But Josefina stood next to the wagon until Papá had finished closing the crate. She wanted to stay near the piano as long as she could. She knew she would never forget the way Tía Dolores's music had sounded, or the way it had made her feel.

When Papá was finished, he saw Josefina. "You liked the piano music, didn't you?" he asked.

"Oh, yes, Papá," answered Josefina. "I didn't want Tía Dolores to stop."

Papá smiled. "I didn't either," he said. "It made me miss playing my violin. Well, there will be plenty of fiddle music at the fandango tonight. You'd better go in now and get ready. The guests will be coming soon."

"Yes, Papá," Josefina answered. She took one last look at the piano crate, then started back inside. As she walked, she thought, *I wish there were some way I could let Tía Dolores know how much I loved the piano music. I wish I could give her something in return. But what?*

Later, when Josefina walked into the back court-yard, she knew the answer to her question. She thought of a fine gift to give Tía Dolores. *I'll give it to her during the fandango tonight*, she decided. She was pleased with her idea. She thought Tía Dolores would be pleased, too.

A Gift for
Tía Dolores

tand still, Josefina," said Francisca. She was slowly and carefully brushing Josefina's hair with a brush made of stiff grasses. Abuelito had brought all four sisters beautiful blue silk hair ribbons. Francisca had put herself in charge of tying them for Josefina and Clara. Josefina fidgeted. She was grateful to Francisca, but she wished she'd *hurry up*. Josefina wanted to be ready for the fandango early, so that she could prepare her gift for Tía Dolores.

Clara tied her sash neatly, then undid it and tied it all over again. Francisca had already brushed Clara's hair and put the blue hair ribbon in it. "Do you think I look all right?" Clara asked.

Josefina and Francisca were surprised. It wasn't like Clara to worry about her appearance. Josefina was afraid Francisca might say something unkind. She was glad when Francisca looked at Clara for a moment and then said seriously, "You look very pretty. The blue suits you."

Clara beamed. She reached up to touch her hair ribbon.

It made Josefina happy to see her sisters getting along. *It's because Tía Dolores is here,* she thought. Francisca and Clara were in complete agreement about Tía Dolores. They both admired her very much. Josefina smiled to herself. Francisca and Clara would be pleased when *they* saw her gift for Tía Dolores, too.

"Finished!" said Francisca. She gave Josefina's ribbon one last adjustment. "You look fine. Use your wings and fly away now, Josefina. I can tell you're anxious to go."

"Gracias, Francisca," Josefina called back over her shoulder as she hurried from the room.

The sun had set. Cool evening air slid down from the mountains, bringing darkness with it. Small bonfires were lit in the front courtyard for light and for warmth. As she crossed the courtyard, Josefina could hear Ana and Carmen thanking some neighbor women who had come early with dishes of food for

the fandango. No one noticed Josefina slip into the
kitchen. She took a small water jar and slipped out
again.

In the back courtyard, Josefina knelt in front of
Mamá's flowers. One by one, she picked all the fresh-
est and brightest-colored flowers. She put them in the
water jar. Josefina was careful to break the flowers off
near the ground so that the stems were long, but she
didn't disturb the roots. There were not very many
flowers, so Josefina had to pick almost all of them in
order to have a bouquet anywhere near big enough and
beautiful enough to give to Tía Dolores.

The corner looked bare when she was through. *It's
all right,* she told herself. *Mamá would approve. After all,
Tía Dolores was the one who sent Mamá the seeds, so Tía
Dolores should be the one to enjoy the flowers. They should
be a gift for her.*

Josefina straightened the flowers in the water jar.
The bouquet looked scrawny somehow. So Josefina
slipped the blue ribbon out of her hair and tied it
around the flowers in a big bow. *There!* she thought
with satisfaction. *That looks much better.* She wanted the
bouquet to be a surprise for everyone, so she looked

around for a place to hide it. She had just entered the narrow passageway between the front and back court-yards when she bumped into Papá.

"What's this you've got here?" asked Papá, peering at Josefina over the tops of the flowers.

"It's . . . they're a gift for Tía Dolores," explained Josefina. "I wanted to give her something to thank her for the music."

It was too dark to see Papá's face clearly, but Josefina could tell by his voice that he was smiling. "I think that is a very fine idea," he said. "I'll tell you what. I am going to make a formal introduction of Tía Dolores to all our friends and neighbors at the fandango tonight. After I do, perhaps you will give Tía Dolores the bouquet."

"Yes, I will!" said Josefina happily.

"Very well," said Papá. "It will be our secret until then."

"Gracias, Papá," said Josefina. After Papá left, Josefina put the jar of flowers under the bench in the passageway. No one would see it there, and she would be able to fetch it quickly when it was time to give it to Tía Dolores.

✿

More guests arrived every moment. They called
out a chorus of greetings to each other as they
crossed the front courtyard to the *gran sala*, the
family's finest room. Because this was a very special
night, the gran sala was lit with candles. Their wavering light made the guests' shadows swoop and dance
on the walls.

Soon the musicians struck up a lively tune on
their fiddles and the real dancing began. It seemed to
Josefina that the dancers flew around the room with
as much ease as their shadows had. Their feet hardly
seemed to touch the floor at all as they whirled by in
a blur of bright colors.

No one whirled faster than Francisca. No one
looked happier or more beautiful. In the candlelight,
her dark curly hair seemed to shine like a black stone
in the stream. And Josefina was glad to see that Ana
had put her responsibilities aside for a while and was
dancing with her husband, Tomás. All around the
sides of the gran sala, older ladies sat holding babies
on their laps so that the babies' young mothers could

dance. The old ladies clapped the babies' hands in time to the music.

Josefina and Clara were still too young to be allowed to dance, so they stood outside in the courtyard and leaned on the windowsill, looking in at the dancers. Josefina's feet danced along to the music. It was impossible to be still! The music seemed to twist and turn in the air, wind its way around all the dancers, and find its way outside to tickle Josefina's feet so that they just had to move.

Every once in a while, over the music and conversation, Josefina and Clara could hear Abuelito's voice. He'd be saying, "*BOOM!* What a sound! Those thieves ran off and I'll bet they're running still." Clara and Josefina grinned at each other. Abuelito was telling the story about Tía Dolores's piano over and over again. The girls noticed that the number of thieves grew larger every time Abuelito told the story!

The person both girls liked best to watch was Tía Dolores. She was easy to pick out of the crowd because she was so tall, and because no one else had hair of quite such a rich, dark red.

"She dances well, doesn't she?" said Clara as

Tía Dolores swept by.

"Yes," said Josefina. "She's as graceful as . . . as the music."

Soon Papá came by the window and nodded to Josefina. Josefina nodded back.

"What's that all about?" asked Clara.

"It's a surprise," said Josefina, excited and smiling. "Stay here and you'll see."

She scurried across the courtyard to the passageway where she'd left the bouquet. It was very dark. Josefina bent down and felt under the bench for the water jar with the bouquet in it. It wasn't there. *That's odd,* she thought.

Josefina stood up, perplexed. And then she saw the jar. It was lying on its side near one wall. It was empty. *Where is the bouquet?* Josefina wondered anxiously.

She looked all around the passageway. The bouquet was nowhere to be seen, but an odd white shape looming in the back courtyard caught her eye. She walked toward it and gasped. Oh, no! The white shape was Florecita! The goat must have broken out of her pen and found her way into the back courtyard.

Josefina did *not* want to put Florecita back in her pen.

When she turned away to get help, she stepped on something. She stooped down and picked it up. At first she didn't know what it was. And then she saw. It was a few green stems held together by a trampled, mud-stained blue ribbon. Suddenly, Josefina realized what had happened. *Florecita had eaten the bouquet!* This was all that was left of the flowers Josefina had picked for Tía Dolores.

But that was not the worst of it. At that instant, Josefina saw what Florecita was doing. Calm as could be, Florecita was standing smack in the middle of what used to be Mamá's flowers. She was chewing a mouthful of stems. One hollyhock, root and all, dangled from her mouth. Josefina could see that no other flowers were left. All that remained were some scraggly, chewed, crushed, and broken stems and a scattering of leaves and petals on the ground.

Florecita turned her nasty yellow eyes on Josefina. The goat looked very satisfied with herself.

Josefina was furious. "Florecita!" she hissed in a ferocious whisper. "You awful, awful animal! You've ruined *everything*."

Josefina was so angry she forgot to be afraid of
Florecita. She marched right up to the goat and yanked
the hollyhock out of her mouth. Florecita looked surprised. She looked even more surprised when Josefina
swatted her on the back with the stems, saying, "How
could you? You ate the bouquet and you killed Mamá's
flowers. Oh, I *hate* you, Florecita!"

Josefina shoved Florecita hard. Then she took hold
of one of Florecita's fearsome horns and pulled with
all her strength. "Come with me," she said. Josefina
dragged Florecita to her pen. She slammed the gate
shut. "I hate you, Florecita," she said again. "I'll hate
you forever!"

Josefina ran all the way back to the bench in the
passageway and slumped down on it. There was nothing to be done. She looked at the dirty blue ribbon and
the chewed stems wilting in her hand and fought back
tears of disappointment.

"Josefina?" a voice said. "What are you doing here
in the darkness?"

Josefina looked up. She saw Tía Dolores coming
toward her. Josefina could hardly talk. She showed the
sad-looking stems to Tía Dolores. "This was a bouquet

for you," she said in a shaky voice. "But our goat Florecita found it and ate it. And she killed Mamá's flowers, too."

"Ah," said Tía Dolores. She sat next to Josefina on the bench.

Slowly, Josefina explained. "I wanted to give you a gift to thank you for the piano music," she said. "So I picked all the best flowers. I tied my new hair ribbon around them. The flowers were so pretty. They grew from the seeds you sent Mamá. I've been watering them since Mamá died, because I know she loved them. Now there are none left. There will never be any more. The flowers are dead."

Tía Dolores was a good listener. She sat still and gave Josefina her full attention. Neither one of them noticed the noise and laughter coming from the gran sala. The fandango seemed far away. When Josefina was finished explaining, Tía Dolores said, "Show me your mamá's flowers."

Josefina led Tía Dolores to the corner of the back courtyard. "You see," she said. "There is nothing left."

Tía Dolores knelt down. She looked at what was left of the flowers. She scooped up a handful of soil and rubbed it between her fingers. Gently, she touched the short, bitten-off stems.

Then she smiled at Josefina. "Don't worry," she said. "Your mamá planted these flowers well. The roots are deep and strong. You've kept them healthy by watering the soil. They'll live, I promise." She stood and brushed the soil off her hands. "Do you like caring for flowers?" she asked.

Josefina nodded. "I used to help Mamá," she said.

"I brought some seeds with me when I left Mexico City," said Tía Dolores. "Perhaps you and I can plant them tomorrow."

"Oh, could we?" said Josefina.

"Yes," said Tía Dolores. "We'll wash your hair ribbon, too. Now we had better go back to the gran sala."

Papá met them at the door. "Josefina," he said. "Where have you been? I introduced Tía Dolores, but then I couldn't find you."

"Oh, Papá," said Josefina. "Florecita ate the bouquet! And then she almost ruined all the rest of Mamá's flowers."

"Ah, that's too bad," said Papá sadly. He looked

around the courtyard. "Is Florecita loose?"

"No," said Josefina. "I dragged her back to her pen and shut the gate."

"You did?" asked Papá. "But I thought you were afraid of Florecita."

"I am," said Josefina. "I mean, I was. I guess just now I was so angry at Florecita I forgot!"

Papá laughed. "Well, we never know where our courage is going to come from!" he said. "I am sorry about the flowers, though."

"Tía Dolores says the flowers will be all right," said Josefina. "She's going to help me plant new seeds tomorrow."

"Is she?" said Papá. He turned and smiled at Tía Dolores. "Well, then, Dolores," he said, "that means you'll have to come back often. You'll have to visit us to see how the flowers are coming along."

"I will," said Tía Dolores. "God willing."

"Come inside and have something to eat now," said Papá. "Ana would never forgive us if we didn't enjoy the food she's prepared."

Josefina followed Papá and Tía Dolores into the gran sala. She grinned to herself. *I guess the caravan didn't need to bring me the courage to stand up to Florecita after all,* she thought. *It turns out I already had it. But I might never have found out if I hadn't picked a bouquet for Tía Dolores.*

An idea danced through Josefina's head just then. As quick as the flicker of starlight on water, the idea appeared and disappeared. But it was an idea that would come again and again all the rest of the night and through the next day, until it grew from an idea into a heartfelt hope.

Josefina's Idea

CHAPTER 4

N ever had Josefina been more eager to begin a day. The next morning she was up even earlier than usual. Quietly, so that she wouldn't waken Francisca or Clara, Josefina rolled up the sheepskins and blankets that were her bed. She dressed and slipped outside. The moon hung low in the sky. It cast such a strong, pure light that everything was bathed in silver or shadow.

Josefina went to the kitchen. Early as it was, Carmen was already there grinding corn for the morning meal. Her husband, Miguel, was starting the kitchen fire. Carmen nodded good morning to Josefina and handed her a water jar to fill at the stream, just as she did every morning. But this morning was different for Josefina. This was the morning of the day Tía Dolores was going to spend with her and her sisters.

48

The huge front gate was closed, so Josefina
stepped through the small door cut into the gate.
She closed the door behind her and ran across the
moon-washed ground to Abuelito's wagon. Standing
on tiptoe, she looked in. There was the big crate with
Tía Dolores's piano inside. Josefina poked her finger
through a crack in the crate and touched the polished
wood of the piano. She smiled when she remembered the pleasure its music had given her. Then she
skipped down to the stream, thinking of the melody
Tía Dolores had played.

The tune stayed in her head as she did her early-
morning chores. She gathered eggs singing it. She
swept the courtyards dancing to it. She piled wood
next to the fireplaces in time to its rhythm. When the
village church bell rang its call to prayers at seven
o'clock, it seemed to ring along with the tune. And
when the family said morning prayers together in front
of the small altar in the family sala, dedicating their
day's work to God, their voices seemed to rise and fall
just as the piano notes had.

The music seemed to be everywhere Josefina went.
Tía Dolores did, too! Tía Dolores was interested in

everything. At breakfast she said, "I want to see as much of the rancho as I can today."

So after breakfast Josefina led Tía Dolores through the orchard, past the cornfields, and to the stream. They filled water jars and carried them up to water the kitchen garden. Then they picked some fat pumpkins for Tía Dolores to take home with her to Santa Fe the next day. "I am sure my mother has no pumpkins as big as these in her garden!" said Tía Dolores.

Wherever she went, Tía Dolores found something to praise. Josefina led Tía Dolores to the weaving room. There Clara showed her the sheep's wool she had carded, spun, and dyed. Tía Dolores admired the colors. "There are no colors finer than these in all of Mexico," she said.

Tía Dolores was a good teacher. She showed Clara a faster way to knit the heel on a sock. She showed Francisca how to sew a patch over a hole so that it hardly showed at all.

Josefina was in the back courtyard clearing away the dead stems Florecita had trampled when Tía Dolores joined her.

"I've brought you some seeds to plant," she said

to Josefina as she handed her a small package.

"Gracias!" said Josefina.

"I'll help you for a while. Then I promised Ana I would make bread with her," said Tía Dolores. She began to dig holes in the soil for the seeds. "Ana has lots of responsibilities, doesn't she?"

"Yes," agreed Josefina. "It's hard for Ana. Mamá ran the household so smoothly. But Ana doesn't always know what to do, and Mamá is not here to teach her."

"Ana is young," said Tía Dolores as she covered some seeds with soil. "It's a good thing she has you and Francisca and Clara to help her."

Josefina nodded slowly. "We try," she said. "But sometimes . . ." She stopped.

Tía Dolores gave her a questioning look.

Josefina sighed. She dug a little hole in the soil. "You see," she said, "Francisca and Clara fight a lot. They are so different! Clara is careful and practical, and Francisca is so quick and fiery. When Mamá was alive, she put a stop to their arguments before they began. But now . . . Well, Ana tries, but she is too soft-hearted and they won't mind her. I try to joke them out of fighting. Sometimes it works. But sometimes it doesn't."

"'Blessed are the peacemakers,'" said Tía Dolores softly, "'for they will be called the children of God.'" She smiled at Josefina. "You know," she said, "it's perfectly natural for sisters to disagree. You should have heard your mamá and me sometimes! She was quite a few years older than I was. I am sure she thought I was a miserable pest. I wanted to be like her. Once I wore her best sash without her permission, and I lost it. Your mamá was very angry. She wouldn't speak to me for days. But she finally forgave me."

Josefina realized suddenly, *Tía Dolores misses her sister. She misses Mamá, too, just as much as we do.* She said, "I wish you could be here to protect these flowers from Florecita when they bloom."

"I'd love to see the flowers," said Tía Dolores. "But *you* can protect them from Florecita. You aren't afraid of her anymore. You don't need me. You will make your mamá's flowers bloom again and keep them safe, Josefina. I know you will."

✦

"Oh, Tía Dolores! It's beautiful!" said Ana. She draped a silk rebozo over her shoulders. Its colors were as bright as flowers. "Gracias!"

It was early afternoon, just after the mid-day meal. Ana, Francisca, Clara, and Josefina were gathered in the family sala. Tía Dolores had called them together. She had presents for them all.

"Francisca," said Tía Dolores. "This is a sewing diary I made for you." She gave Francisca a little hand-made book. "There are sketches of dresses in it, and samples of material, and notes about how to make the dresses."

"Gracias!" said Francisca. Eagerly, she looked at the sewing diary. "The dresses are so elegant, Tía Dolores!" she said. "I wish you could be here to help us make them." She looked up and joked, "I'm afraid I will sew a sleeve on upside down!"

"The notes and directions will help you," said Tía Dolores.

Francisca looked doubtful. "But I can't read," she said. "None of us can."

"Oh!" said Tía Dolores. "Well, then! Just use your good sense. I am sure if you and your sisters help each other, you will do very well."

For Clara, Tía Dolores had brought a fine pair of

scissors and some sewing needles. Clara was very pleased, because her gift was beautiful *and* useful.

"And this is for you, Josefina," said Tía Dolores. She handed Josefina a necklace. A small, dark red stone surrounded by gold hung from a delicate chain.

Josefina smiled. The necklace was lovely. "Gracias, Tía Dolores," she said. Her hands were shaky with excitement as she put the necklace on.

"My!" said Francisca. "Isn't that necklace quite grown-up?"

"Yes, indeed it is," said Tía Dolores firmly. "And isn't Josefina quite grown-up, too?"

Francisca said no more.

"Tía Dolores," said Ana. "How did you know what would be the perfect gift for each one of us?"

Tía Dolores smiled. "All the years I lived in Mexico City, I looked forward to the caravans coming," she said. "I knew Abuelito would bring stories about all of you and your life here on the rancho. Sometimes he would bring a letter dictated by your mamá. I felt as if I were watching you grow up even though I was far away. When I decided to come home, I enjoyed thinking about what present to bring each of you."

"Well," said Ana. "I'm sorry we didn't know that you were coming. We have nothing to give you in return for your gifts."

"Oh," laughed Tía Dolores. "This day with you is all the gift I want."

When the afternoon had cooled into early evening, Tía Dolores and Abuelito walked to the village. They wanted to say a prayer at Mamá's grave. They were also going to visit Papá's oldest sister, who lived in the village.

Josefina and her sisters sat in a corner of the front courtyard that was still warm from the heat of the day's sun. Every now and then they could hear Ana's little boys laughing with Carmen in the kitchen nearby. The sisters were peeling back the husks from roasted ears of corn. They were going to braid the husks together to make a long string of ears so that the corn could be hung out to dry.

Josefina said, "Hasn't it been nice today, having Tía Dolores here?"

"Yes!" said Ana. "She was such a help to me! And she was so kind to my little boys."

"Tía Dolores is a very sensible, hardworking

person," said Clara. That was her highest praise.

"Oh, Clara!" protested Francisca. "You make her sound as dull as these ears of corn! I found her to be elegant and graceful."

Josefina decided the time had come to tell her sisters her idea. She picked up an ear of corn and peeled the husk slowly. "What if," she said quietly, "we asked Tía Dolores to stay?"

No one said anything. They were all too surprised.

Josefina went on. "She could help us and teach us, the way she did today."

"She wouldn't stay," said Francisca. "She's used to life in Mexico City, where there are lots of grand people and grand houses. She doesn't want to live on a rancho."

"But she said she always loved to hear about the rancho when Abuelito came to visit her, remember?" said Josefina. "And she doesn't act fancy or put on airs. She likes it here. She was interested in everything."

"Yes," said Ana. "But I think perhaps she has come home hoping to get married and start a family of her own. She's not too old for that, you know."

"She wouldn't have to stay here forever," said Josefina. "Just for a few months. And anyway, she is our aunt. We *are* her family."

Clara picked up several ears of corn and put them in her lap. "Well," she said in her flat, no-nonsense manner. "Even if Tía Dolores would be willing to stay, it wouldn't be proper for us to ask her. Papá would have to approve of the idea. He would have to be the one to ask her to stay."

Josefina's heart sank. She hadn't thought of that. She knew Clara was right.

"Who wants to be the one to present the idea to Papá?" Clara asked. "I certainly don't." She turned to Josefina. "It's your idea," she said. "Do you want to talk to Papá about it?"

Josefina looked down at the ear of corn in her hands. "No," she said in a small voice.

"Will you go to him, Ana?" Clara asked. "You are the oldest."

"Oh, I couldn't!" said Ana. "Papá might think I was complaining. If I say that I need Tía Dolores's help, he might think I don't want to do what it is my responsibility to do."

"Oh!" exclaimed Francisca. She stood up and brushed off her skirt. "*I'm* not afraid to talk to Papá.

I'll just march right up to him and say, 'Papá! You must ask Tía Dolores to stay!'"

Ana, Clara, and Josefina looked at each other. They knew that was not at all the right way to speak to Papá! It wasn't that Papá was stern or cold. But he was the *patrón*, the head of the rancho and the head of their family. The girls had never presented such an important idea to him before. It would have to be done politely and with respect.

"Wait, Francisca!" said Josefina. She stood up, too. "I think all of us should speak to Papá. We should go together. That way Papá will see that all four of us would like Tía Dolores to stay."

Ana and Clara didn't move.

"Come on," said Josefina. She grinned. "Don't worry. I'll do the talking if you don't want to. Last night I had the courage to stand up to Florecita. Papá is much, much kinder than *she* is!"

The sisters found Papá near the animal pens. He was tightening the latch on the gate.

He smiled when he saw Josefina. "The latch is stronger now," he said. "We shouldn't have any more goats in Mamá's flowers."

"That's good!" said Josefina. She swallowed. Francisca gave her a little shove forward. "Papá," Josefina said. "May we ask you something?"

Papá looked at the four girls. "Yes?" he said.

"Do you think," Josefina said carefully, "that you could ask Tía Dolores to stay here with us for a while?"

"Ask her to stay?" repeated Papá.

"Yes," said Josefina. "Not forever, just for a while. She could help us. And she could teach us, the way . . . the way Mamá did. Please, would you ask her?"

Josefina saw a look of sadness cross Papá's face. He turned away. "I'll consider it," he said.

"But Papá," Francisca blurted. "You must—"

Josefina tugged on Francisca's sleeve and frowned at her to make her stop talking.

"Gracias, Papá," said Josefina. She hesitated, and then she added, "We need Tía Dolores."

Then she and her sisters left.

✳

"What do you think Papá will do?" Francisca whispered. She and Clara and Josefina were in their sleeping sala, getting ready for bed. "Do you think he will speak to Tía Dolores?"

"I don't know," said Josefina. "I hope so."

"And if he does ask her, what do you think she will say?" Francisca wondered aloud.

Josefina sighed. "I don't know," she said again.

"I think you're silly to wonder about it," Clara said. "We'll find out tomorrow. Abuelito and the caravan will leave first thing in the morning. Tía Dolores will either leave with him or not. We'll just have to wait and see."

"Oh! I hate waiting!" said Francisca.

The three sisters smiled at each other. They all hated to wait! On that they certainly agreed!

The next morning, they were up early. Even Francisca, who was usually slow getting dressed, was ready and waiting with Ana, Clara, and Josefina next to Abuelito's wagon. They watched the servants load Abuelito's small trunk onto the wagon.

Then, with sinking hearts, the sisters saw Tía Dolores's trunk loaded onto the wagon as well.

"Papá didn't ask her!" Francisca groaned.

"Or maybe he did, and she said no," said Ana.

"She doesn't want to stay," Clara added.

Josefina was so disappointed she couldn't talk.
A lump rose in her throat when she heard Papá and
Tía Dolores and Abuelito coming. Suddenly, Josefina
didn't want to stand there by the wagon one second
longer. She couldn't bear to kiss Tía Dolores and
Abuelito good-bye.

Without a murmur, she slipped away, back inside
the house. She went to the gran sala because it was the
only room that was sure to be empty. As she walked
into the cool darkness of the gran sala, she remembered
how it had looked the night of the fandango, full of life
and music. Now there was nothing but shadows.

Just then, in a corner of the room, Josefina saw a
large, dark shape. She caught her breath when she saw
what it was.

It was Tía Dolores's piano. Instantly, Josefina knew
what that meant. Tía Dolores would never have left her
piano, unless . . .

Josefina flew across the courtyard and out the front
gate so fast it seemed as if she had wings on her feet.
Tía Dolores caught her in her arms.

"There you are, Josefina!" Tía Dolores said. "I
wanted to say good-bye to you."

Josefina pulled back and looked at Tía Dolores's face. "I'm going to Santa Fe," Tía Dolores said. "I'm going to see my dear mamá, whom I have not seen for ten years. But then I'll come back."

"When?" asked Josefina.

Tía Dolores laughed. "Soon," she said. "And when I come back, I'll stay as long as you need me."

Josefina hugged Tía Dolores hard. Then Tía Dolores swung herself up onto the wagon.

"Well, well, well," said Abuelito. He pretended to be cross. "Now it seems that if I want to see Dolores, I'm going to have to come here and see all of you girls, too. What a bother! What a bother!" He sighed. "At least I don't have to carry that piano with me today. Though if we meet up with any thieves, I'll just have to frighten them off with my singing, I suppose!"

Then he kissed Josefina and her sisters good-bye and gave them his blessing.

"*Adiós*, Abuelito!" called all the girls as the wagon pulled away. "Adiós, Tía Dolores."

"Come back soon!" Josefina sang out as she waved good-bye.

As soon as the wagon was out of sight, Josefina

hurried back inside. She went to the kitchen to get a jar. She wanted to fill the jar with water to sprinkle on Mamá's flowers.

Tía Dolores will be back soon, she thought. *I want the flowers to be beautiful when she returns!*

Josefina set off for the stream, whistling Tía Dolores's tune.

Light and Shadow

he month that Tía Dolores was away felt very long to Josefina. She missed her aunt every minute that she was gone. But Tía Dolores had kept her promise, and after visiting her parents in Santa Fe, she returned to the rancho with her servant Teresita in time to help with the harvest. Tía Dolores had been back for two weeks now, and Josefina was glad.

"María Josefina Montoya!" Tía Dolores said happily. It was a rainy night in October, and Josefina and her sisters were sewing in front of the fire in the family sala. "How beautiful you look!"

Josefina blushed and smiled at her aunt. "Gracias," she said. She smoothed the long skirt of her new dress with both hands. The cotton material felt soft and light. Josefina rose up on her toes and spun, just for the sheer pleasure of it. She was very proud of her dress, which she had just finished hemming. She had never had a dress made in this elegant new high-waisted style before. Tía Dolores had given Josefina and each of her sisters some material. Josefina's material was a pretty yellow, with narrow stripes and tiny berries on it. She had cut her material carefully, the way Mamá had taught her. Then, stitch by tiny stitch, she had sewn her dress together all by herself. Now, as she spun around, the hearth fire cast a pattern of light and shadow swooping across the dress like a flock of fluttering birds.

Josefina stopped spinning and sighed with peaceful contentment. She was grateful for the fire's warmth as well as its cheerful brightness. A steady, heavy rain was falling outside, but inside it was cozy. The thick, white-washed *adobe* walls kept out the cold and took on a rosy glow from the firelight.

Tía Dolores sat next to Clara. "Don't use such a long thread in your needle," she advised Clara gently. "It might tangle."

Josefina grinned. "Remember, Clara?" she said. "Mamá used to say, 'If you make your thread too long, the devil will catch on to the end of it!'"

All the sisters smiled and nodded, and Tía Dolores said, "I remember your mamá saying that to me when we were young girls learning to sew!"

Tía Dolores was smiling. But Josefina saw that her eyes were sad, and she knew that Tía Dolores was missing Mamá.

Josefina and her sisters thought of Mamá every day, with longing and love. Every day, the girls tried to do their chores the way Mamá had taught them to. They tried to be as respectful, hardworking, and obedient as she would have wished them to be. Every day, they recalled her wise and funny sayings and songs. And every day, they remembered her in their prayers.

As Clara shortened her thread, she looked at Josefina's dress. "You'll get a lot of good wear out of that dress," she said, sounding sensible as usual. "It was a good idea to make it too long. That way you can grow into it."

"Oh, dear!" said Josefina, looking at her hem. "Is my dress too long?"

"Not at all. It's perfect," said Ana in her tender-hearted way. "You've done a fine job, Josefina. And you are the first one of us to finish." Ana had not even begun her dress yet. She had decided to make vests for her two little boys first.

Francisca sighed a huge sigh. "I'm far from finishing my dress," she said. "I've still so much to do."

"You shouldn't have chosen such a fancy dress pattern," said Clara, pricking her material with the sharp needle. The sewing diary that Tía Dolores had given Francisca showed all the latest styles from Mexico City, and the girls had each chosen a dress pattern to follow. Clara was making a dress that was plain and simple. She prided herself on being practical and often felt called upon to point it out when someone else wasn't. That someone was usually Francisca.

Francisca had chosen an elaborate pattern from the sewing diary. She'd begun enthusiastically. She cut into the material boldly, talking all the while about how splendid her dress would be. But the long, slow work of sewing the pieces together bored Francisca. She complained with every stitch. "I'll never finish my dress," she said now, "unless someone helps me with this endless stitching." She glanced sideways at Tía Dolores.

Josefina saw the sideways look. She knew that

Francisca wanted Tía Dolores to sew for her. But Tía
Dolores calmly continued her own sewing. She said
nothing, even when Francisca sighed loudly again.
Josefina was not surprised. In the last two weeks, she
had learned that Tía Dolores was always willing to give
help and advice. But she would not do the girls' work
for them.

A few days ago, Josefina and Tía Dolores had
worked together in the corner of the back courtyard
where Mamá's flowers grew. Tía Dolores showed
Josefina how to prepare the flowers for the winter. She
explained how to cut back the dead stems and cover
the earth with leaves to protect it from ice and snow.
She watched with care to be sure Josefina was doing
everything correctly. Tía Dolores helped, but she made
it clear that the flowers were Josefina's responsibility.
"I want you to know how to care for them by yourself
after I leave," she'd said. "I know you can do it. I have
faith in you."

Tía Dolores worked hard teaching, and she
expected the girls to work hard learning. "Our ener-
gies and abilities are gifts from God," she often said.
"He means for us to put them to good use." Sometimes

Josefina thought that perhaps Tía Dolores had a little too *much* faith in her abilities! As soon as she'd returned to the rancho, Tía Dolores had had her piano moved into the family sala. The piano had come all the way from Mexico City, and Josefina was eager to learn how to play it. So Tía Dolores gave Josefina lessons. Right away, Josefina had learned that making music on the piano was much harder than it looked. But Tía Dolores was generous with her encouragement. She never gave up, no matter how Josefina fumbled at the keys.

Now Francisca frowned and rustled her material. She made a great show of holding it up to the fire and squinting as she stitched. Clara glanced at the hem Francisca was sewing. "Just look at the size of your stitches!" she said. "They're much too big."

Francisca shrugged. "They'll hold the dress together," she said.

"That's not the point," said Clara. "They *look* bad."

"Oh, Clara!" said Francisca crossly. "The stitches are on the inside! No one will see them."

"Yes, they will!" said Josefina, who didn't like to hear her sisters squabble. "No one's dress swirls more than yours at a dance, Francisca. And no one is more admired!" Josefina whirled around the room, pretending to be Francisca dancing. "See my hem stitches?" she asked. She sang a dancing song that had been one of Mamá's favorites.

Tía Dolores knew the song, too. She went straight to the piano and began to play it. Ana and Clara sang along and clapped in time to the music. Francisca tried not to smile. But when Josefina danced over to her, holding out both hands, Francisca happily thrust her sewing aside and sprang to her feet. Josefina and Francisca danced around the room, weaving in and out of the light of the fire. Soon Ana and Clara were dancing with each other, too. Tía Dolores played away merrily. Her rebozo slipped down from her shoulders. Her dark, shiny hair had a reddish luster in the firelight.

Tía Dolores was playing so loudly and they were all singing and laughing so much that none of them heard the door open. But it must have, because the next thing Josefina knew, Papá was there, tapping his foot in time to Tía Dolores's music. He watched the girls dance until the song was over. When they stopped, he folded his arms across his chest and pretended to scold.

"Dancing instead of sewing?" he asked. He tried to look stern, but his eyes were full of fun. "Who started that fandango?"

"I did, Papá!" said Josefina, flushed and breathless. "I was celebrating. I've finished my dress!"

"Good!" said Papá. "And a fine dress it is, too."

"Gracias, Papá," said Josefina. She held out the sides of her dress. "The material comes from very far away. Tía Dolores gave it to us."

"How thoughtful of her," said Papá. He turned to Tía Dolores. "You are very kind to my daughters. Gracias."

Tía Dolores looked pleased. "My father bought the material this summer from traders who came to Santa Fe from the United States. The traders brought all sorts of things to trade—tools and clothes, paper and ink—"

"And pretty material!" Josefina added happily.

"*Sí,*" said Papá. "I know about the *americanos* and the trail they follow. They first came to Santa Fe three years ago. Before that, it was illegal for them to come to New Mexico." He looked thoughtful. "I hope that trading with the americanos will be a good thing. I've heard that the traders need pack mules, so I'm raising some to take to Santa Fe next summer. I'll sell or swap the mules to get tools and other things we need on the rancho. It should be a profitable business."

"Oh, Papá," Josefina asked, "may we go to Santa Fe with you next summer?"

"Perhaps," said Papá, smiling at her eagerness. "But right now, I think all of you girls had better go to bed. I'm going to the village."

"In this storm?" asked Ana.

"It's because of the storm that I'm going," said Papá as he put on his hat. "I want to be sure Magdalena is all right." Tía Magdalena was Papá's sister. She was much older than he was, and she lived alone in the village about a mile from the rancho. "Her roof is not as strong as it should be, and her house is near the stream. I'm worried about flooding. Most of the time, nothing is more welcome than rain. But it's unusual for it to rain so late in the year, and such a hard rain can mean trouble."

Josefina listened. They'd been making so much noise, they hadn't noticed that the wind had an angry sound to it now, and the rain was coming down harder and harder. She watched Papá as he pulled on his woolen *sarape* that covered his chest and his back. Even that wouldn't keep him dry tonight. Josefina turned a worried face up to Papá.

"Now, now. There's no need for you to worry, my Josefina," Papá said in his deep, comforting voice. "Our house is high above the stream. God will keep you safe, and your Tía Dolores is here to look after you."

"Sí, Papá," said Josefina. "But if the stream floods—"

"Our harvest is safely in," said Papá. "We'll move the animals to higher ground if we need to. Now come and say good night to me before I go."

The girls knelt before Papá, the palms and fingers of their hands pressed together as for prayer. Papá gave each girl his blessing and kissed her praying hands. His smile was loving as he looked down on his daughters' upturned faces. "Go to bed," he said. "The sky will be blue tomorrow."

Tía Dolores opened the door for Papá. "God go with you," she said softly.

Papá nodded. Then he went out into the windy, rainy night.

✳

Papá had told Josefina not to worry, but she could not obey. The sheepskins that were her bed were warm and soft and comforting, but they could not soothe away the worry that kept her awake. She lay on her stomach with her chin on her clenched hands and listened. Moment by moment the wind grew wilder. It shrieked and howled and hurled the rain against the roof and the walls as if it were trying to destroy the house with its anger. Josefina shivered at the sound of the storm's rage. *Please let Papá be safe,* she prayed. *Please.* She was glad she couldn't sleep. She hoped her prayers would protect Papá.

And so, when the church bell rang in the night, Josefina was already awake. The bell's fast *clang, clang, clang* came through the storm's uneven gusts. It was faint but steady. Josefina knew the church bell was an alarm. Its clangs meant *danger, danger, danger!*

"Francisca! Clara!" said Josefina urgently. "Wake up!" She stood and began to put on her clothes.

Francisca groaned and pulled her blankets over her head, but Clara sat up straight. "What's the matter?" she asked Josefina.

"The church bell is ringing," said Josefina. "Hurry!

Get dressed. Papá may need our help."

The sisters dressed as fast as they could. Just as they were finishing, Tía Dolores came to fetch them. She was carrying a small candle. Her voice was calm and very serious. She spoke against the sounds of the storm with the same steady determination as the ringing church bell. "Your papá is still down in the village. I fear the church bell means the flooding is bad there. I've wakened all the workers in the house. Some will herd the animals to higher ground. Others will try to build up the stream's banks so that the stream won't flood the fields. I've told Ana she must stay with her boys. But I want you girls to come with me. We must save as much as we can from the kitchen garden."

Josefina, Clara, and Francisca followed Tía Dolores. They were still under the cover of the roof when suddenly the sky was slashed in two by a jagged dagger of lightning. Its brilliant flash of light made everything white for a second. Then the light disappeared and the night seemed even darker than before. BOOM! A huge clap of thunder crashed so loudly it shook the house. Josefina stepped back, trembling.

"What's the matter?" Tía Dolores asked.

"It's the lightning," Francisca answered. "Josefina's afraid of it."

CRACK! Lightning split the sky again. Josefina couldn't move. All her life she had feared lightning. Mamá had understood. She would hug Josefina to her and wrap her rebozo around both of them. She'd cover Josefina's eyes with her hand so that Josefina wouldn't have to see the wicked flash of light or the plunge into darkness that followed. She'd hold Josefina so close that the beating of her heart almost blocked out the sound of the thunder. *Mamá!* thought Josefina now, bracing herself for another flash. *Help me!*

Just then, Josefina felt Tía Dolores put a strong arm around her shoulders. Tía Dolores's little candle sputtered wildly in the wind, but it didn't go out. By its feeble light, Josefina saw Tía Dolores's gentle face. "Come with me, Josefina," she said.

Josefina took a shaky breath. She leaned close to Tía Dolores. Together, they stepped forward. Clara and Francisca followed behind. The rain put the little candle out. But Tía Dolores's step was sure, even in the darkness. She led the girls across the front court-yard, through the passageway, and into the back courtyard. As they passed Mamá's flowers, Josefina remembered what Tía Dolores had said when they'd worked together: *I know you can do it. I have faith in you.* Lightning sliced the sky and thunder boomed, again and again. Josefina shuddered, but Tía Dolores's arm gave her courage. She stayed within its safe hold as they went out the back gate to the kitchen garden.

Carmen, the cook, and her husband, Miguel, were already there filling big baskets with squash, beans, chiles, and pumpkins. The kitchen garden was awash in mud. It made Josefina sad to see it. She and her sisters had worked so hard all spring and summer tending the garden! She was sorry to pick the squash that were not perfectly ripe yet, but she knew it was better than letting them be washed away or rot from lying in water.

And there was so *much* water! A river of it rushed through the center of the garden, and the rain was still falling in torrents. Mud pulled at Josefina's moccasins and splashed up onto her legs. Soon she was soaked to the skin. Her hands were numb with cold and caked with dirt. Her arms were tired from lifting mud-streaked pumpkins, and her back hurt from carrying her heavy basket. Lightning flashed all around her and thunder rumbled. But Josefina bent to her work, trying to ignore the force and fury of the storm.

Tía Dolores has faith in me, Josefina said to herself. *I can't let her down.*

Turning Blankets into Sheep

ust as Papá had promised, the sky was a clean, clear blue the next morning. Only a few gray clouds remained, and they scuttled across the horizon as if they were ashamed, shoving against each other in their hurry to get away. Below, the ground was so wet it was shiny, reflecting the new blue sky. It was crisscrossed everywhere with thin little rivers no bigger than trickles, trying to find their way down the hill back to the stream.

Papá had come home from the village at dawn, just in time for morning prayers. As she'd knelt in front of the altar in the family sala, Josefina had thanked God for Papá's safe return.

Now the family was gathered in the kitchen for breakfast. Josefina was helping Clara and Carmen cook tortillas. Ana was rocking her younger boy,

Antonio, in a cradle that swung gently from the ceiling. Francisca was grinding corn. She would put a handful of dried corn on the flat *metate* stone and rub back and forth with the smaller *mano* stone until the corn was ground into coarse flour. As the cradle swung back and forth, it made a comforting *creak, creak, creak* sound, which the soft, regular *thud, thud, thud* of the mano matched in rhythm.

Papá looked tired. Tía Dolores gave him some mint tea. He sat down and took a long, grateful sip before he spoke.

"You all did a fine job of saving as much as you could from the garden," he said. "I'm afraid the news from the village is not as good. I was in time to save Magdalena's roof, but one whole corner of the church collapsed. Some of the villagers had not harvested yet, so their crops are lost. They were swept away by the stream when it rose over its banks."

"What a blessing it is that you brought our harvest in early!" said Ana. "We'll be able to share it with the villagers who lost their crops. No one will go hungry this winter."

"Sí," said Papá. "That is a blessing." He paused as

if he didn't want to say what he had to say next. At last
he said sadly, "But we've suffered another loss. I was
told about it late last night. It seems that the shepherds
were moving our sheep from their summer grazing
lands in the mountains down to the winter pastures
closer to the rancho. When the storm began, the shepherds took a shortcut to save time. Just as they were
crossing the bottom of a deep *arroyo*, a flash flood
came gushing through it. All of a sudden, the arroyo
was full of a raging torrent of water. The water came
so hard and so fast that the sheep couldn't get out of
its way. The shepherds risked their lives to save as
many sheep as they could. But hundreds of our sheep
were drowned." As if he needed to hear it again to
believe it, Papá repeated, "Hundreds of our sheep were
drowned."

Ana lifted Antonio out of the cradle and held him
close. Everyone else was still. They looked at Papá,
their faces full of concern. Then Josefina went to stand
by Papá's side. She put her hand on his arm and he
patted it while he stared into the fire. So many sheep
killed! Josefina knew that this was a terrible disaster.
How cruel the storm had been! The rancho could not

survive without sheep. They provided meat, and wool for weaving and for trading. What would Papá do?

Papá's voice was heavy with discouragement. "The sheep were very valuable," he said. "My father and grandfather built up the flocks over many years. It will take a long, long time for us to recover from this loss." He sighed. "We'll just have to start over. I'll have to trade the mules I was raising. I have nothing else to trade. I'll have to use the mules to get new sheep so that we can increase our flocks again."

"Perhaps not," said Tía Dolores. She'd been so quiet, they'd almost forgotten she was there. Now she spoke to Papá, respectfully but firmly. "Forgive me for speaking, but perhaps it won't be necessary to trade the mules. Perhaps you could use the old sheep to get new sheep."

They all stared at her. "Please go on," said Papá.

Tía Dolores explained. "The old sheep provided you with sacks and sacks of wool when they were sheared last spring," she said. "Your storerooms are full of their fleece. What if we used that wool to weave as many blankets as we can? We'll keep as few as possible for our own use, and trade most of the blankets to the

villagers for new sheep. We can trade with the Indians
at the pueblo, too."

"But they all weave their own blankets," said Papá.
"Why would they want more?"

"To trade to the americanos," answered Tía Dolores.
"My father told me that the americanos are glad to
trade their goods for blankets. They value the blankets
for their warmth and strength and beauty."

"I don't understand," said Francisca. "Who will do
all of this weaving you talk about?"

Tía Dolores smiled. "We will," she said. "You and
your sisters and I. The household servants will weave,
and any workers on the rancho who are able."

Josefina saw that Francisca wasn't pleased with
this answer, and Clara and Ana looked unsure. But
Papá seemed to be giving the idea grave consideration.
"Trading blankets for sheep," he said thoughtfully.
"Perhaps it would be good for both sides. Our neigh-
bors would help us by giving us the sheep we need.
And *we* would help *them* by weaving blankets they can
trade for goods that they need."

"Sí," said Tía Dolores simply.

Ana nudged Josefina with her elbow and raised her

eyebrows. None of the sisters had ever heard Papá discuss business with a woman before. He was the patrón, the head of the rancho and the head of their family. He had never discussed business with Mamá. But Papá didn't seem to be offended by Tía Dolores's forwardness. Still, Josefina was not sure it was proper for Tía Dolores to have such a conversation with him. Josefina knew she and her sisters should sit quietly. They all knew it wasn't their place to speak.

All except Francisca, of course. "But Tía Dolores!" Francisca protested. "I don't see how we can weave any more than we already do! We hardly have time to do all our household chores as it is."

"We'll get up earlier," said Tía Dolores briskly. "If all four of you help—"

"Josefina can't help," said Francisca. "She doesn't know how to weave."

Ana nodded, and even Clara agreed with Francisca for once. "That's true," Clara said. "Mamá never taught her, because Josefina was too small. She's *still* too small to work the big loom."

"My servant, Teresita, weaves on a smaller loom that hangs from the ceiling," said Tía Dolores. "I'm sure she'd be willing to teach Josefina to weave on one like it. And I'm sure Josefina is big enough to do it. Josefina can help."

Josefina saw Papá looking at her. His smile said that he loved her even if he wasn't sure she could be of help with the weaving. With all her heart, Josefina wanted to please Papá. She could tell that Tía Dolores's idea had caught his interest and given him a little hope. She didn't want her sisters' doubts to discourage Papá—or Tía Dolores. And so she spoke up with spirit.

"I'd like to learn to use the small loom," she said. "And anyway, I can help wash and card and spin wool for the big loom. I know where to find the plants we use to make dye to color the wool, and . . . and Mamá always used to say that I was good at untangling knots."

Papá laughed out loud. His laugh was a sudden, unexpected, wonderful sound. "Well," he said to Tía Dolores. "If all of your weavers are as eager as my little Josefina, you'll turn the wool into blankets and the blankets into sheep in no time! I think we should give your plan a try."

Tía Dolores was very pleased. "We will pray for God's help," she said, "as we put His gifts to good use. Won't we, girls?"

Her smile was so happy, so full of energy and encouragement, that all the sisters had to smile back and say "Sí!" Even Francisca!

That very afternoon, Tía Dolores brought Josefina to Teresita. "Will you teach Josefina to weave?" she asked.

Teresita was working at a loom that hung near one wall and stretched from ceiling to floor. She looked at Josefina, and then she smiled. Teresita's smile seemed to use her whole face, because her eyes were surrounded by wrinkles of good humor. "Sí," she said.

"Gracias," said Tía Dolores. "You might as well begin right now. As I always say, 'The saints cry over lost time.'"

She left, and Teresita watched her go with a twinkle in her eye. Josefina could tell that she and Teresita were thinking the same thing—that Tía Dolores gave the saints very little reason to cry! She never wasted time!

Josefina sat down next to Teresita and watched her weave. After a little while Josefina asked, "How did you learn to weave?"

Teresita's voice was unhurried as she answered. "Before I came here with your Tía Dolores, I was a servant in your Abuelito's house in Santa Fe," she said. "But when I was a little girl, I lived with my people, the Navajos. My mamá taught me to weave on a loom like this. I've never forgotten, even though I was captured by enemies of the Navajos when I was about your age and taken from my family."

Josefina knew that the Navajo Indians lived in the mountains and deserts far to the west. "Did you ever see your mamá again?" she asked Teresita.

"No," said Teresita.

"Did you miss her?" asked Josefina.

"Sí," said Teresita. Her dark eyes met Josefina's. "You and I are alike in that way, aren't we?" she said. "We both lost our mamás at a young age."

Josefina nodded.

"I am sure you remember the things your mamá taught you," said Teresita.

Josefina nodded again. "Oh, sí!" she said. "My

sisters and I try very hard to remember her lessons and stories and songs."

"Good," said Teresita. She was quiet for a long moment. With a light touch, she ran her hand across the loom. Then she said, "Here is a story my mamá told me. When the world was new, Spider Woman taught the Navajos to weave on a loom like this one. The upper crosspiece is the sky bar. The lower cross-piece is the earth bar, and this stick, which goes between the strands of yarn, is a sunbeam. I'll show you how it works."

Josefina watched. The loom looked like a tall harp. Long, taut strands of wool yarn connected the sky bar to the earth bar. The sunbeam stick held the strands apart. It made space between the strands so that Teresita could weave another piece of wool through them. When she had woven the wool through all the long strands, Teresita pulled the wool gently, pushed it down into place, then turned it and wove it back in the other direction. Teresita's hands made it look easy. Josefina could not wait to try. "May I do it?" she asked.

Teresita handed her the wool. "Remember," she said, "the earth, the sky, and the sun have already

worked hard to provide us with this wool by growing
grass for the sheep to eat. They didn't hurry their work,
and neither should you."

Josefina worked very slowly indeed, but even
so, the row she wove was loose and bumpy. Teresita
helped her take it out and do it over again.

Josefina was weaving a straight row that was a pale
gray color. But the part of the blanket that Teresita had
woven had a lovely pattern of stripes and zigzagging
lines and diamond shapes and triangles on it. The dark
blue zigzags reminded Josefina of the mountains that
surrounded the rancho, and the creamy white zigzags
just above them looked like the snow that capped the
mountains. Floating below the zigzag mountains were
dark V's that looked just like the graceful wild geese
Josefina saw flying across the autumn sky. And below
them, Teresita had woven pale golden shapes that
reminded Josefina of the cottonwood leaves that fell all
around her when she went to the stream every morning. Most of the colors of the blanket were soft—deep
browns, many gentle shades of gray and blue, and delicate gold and yellow. But every few rows, Teresita had
woven in a yarn that was the fiery orange-red of the

harvest moon. "The pattern is so pretty," said Josefina. "It reminds me of our rancho."

"Yes," said Teresita, wrinkling up her eyes in a smile. "A blanket should be as beautiful as the place it comes from." She was thoughtful for a while before she said, "Maybe this blanket will travel all the way to the United States. Maybe some little girl there will look at it, and then she will know how beautiful it is here in New Mexico."

Josefina liked that idea. "She'll probably like the red strands the best," she said, "just as I do. They stand out from all the rest."

"They do," said Teresita. "But every strand, dull or bright, is part of the pattern. Every strand adds to the strength and beauty of the whole blanket."

"Sí," agreed Josefina. "But the red wool seems to change everything around it somehow. It makes all the colors look better."

That first day, Josefina had to do her row of weaving over and over again before it was smooth and even. But Teresita was very patient, and slowly, slowly, Josefina's hands became accustomed to the feeling of the wool. When Josefina came for her next weaving lesson, Teresita had set up a loom for her to use by herself.

Josefina enjoyed her weaving lessons with Teresita. It was a pleasure to weave the wool through the strands, and to push the newly woven row down so that it fit snugly next to the row below it. Part of the pleasure was knowing that with each row, Josefina was adding to a blanket that would help Papá replace the sheep he'd lost. Josefina was pleased and proud to be of help to her family. And as the days went by and she learned to be a better weaver, she was pleased and proud of herself for learning something new. *I may be the youngest and the smallest, but I can help, just like my sisters,* she thought. *I can help turn blankets into sheep! Tía Dolores was right.*

Sometimes as she was weaving, Josefina smiled to herself, thinking of Tía Dolores. It seemed to Josefina that Tía Dolores was like the beautiful bright red wool. She changed everything around her and made it better.

Rabbit Brush

ollow me!" Josefina shouted happily. She ran up the hill as swift and light as a bird skimming over a stream. The air at the top smelled of spicy juniper and piney *piñón*. It was pure and cool and thin and sweet. Josefina turned around and called back to her sisters, "Wait till you see! There's *lots* of rabbit brush up here!"

Josefina and her sisters were on an expedition to gather wildflowers, herbs, roots, barks, berries, and leaves. They'd use them to make dyes to color the wool for weaving. Teresita had told Josefina that the Navajos used rabbit brush blossoms to make many shades of yellow. Ana, Francisca, and Clara were not far behind Josefina on the path. Josefina was glad it was almost time for the mid-day meal. She knew that Carmen had packed tortillas, onions, squash, goat cheese, and

plums for them to eat. The canteen was full of cold
water to drink. Miguel, Carmen's husband, was carrying the food and the canteen. He had come along to be
sure the girls were safe.

"Oh!" said Ana when she reached the top of the hill.
"Isn't it pretty up here!" Josefina thought Ana looked
very pretty herself! She was a little breathless, and her
cheeks were reddened by the climb and the wind.

All the sisters seemed to be in high spirits. They set
to work gathering rabbit brush, delighted to be out in
the bracing air and bright sunshine. Clara, who usually
liked to keep her feet firmly on the ground, seemed to
have a bounce in her step today. And Francisca, who
was usually so careful of her appearance, didn't seem
to care that her hair was windblown and tousled and
had a yellow leaf caught in it.

"Look," said Josefina. She took the leaf out of
Francisca's hair and twirled it on its stem. The leaf was
such a sunny yellow, Josefina thought about saving it
to put in her memory box along with the pretty swallow's feather she'd found earlier. She kept things that
reminded her of Mamá in her memory box. Mamá had
loved swallows, and she had loved autumn, too, when

the bright yellow leaves stood out against the dark green of the mountainsides and shimmered against the deep blue sky. But Josefina knew that the little leaf would soon turn brown and crumble, so she let it go. She watched the breeze catch it and send it swooping and flying as if it were a tiny yellow bird.

Josefina loved autumn as much as Mamá had. It was a busy time on the rancho. All the harvested crops had to be stored properly to preserve them for the winter. The storeroom was full of garlic, onions, beans, corn, squash, pumpkins, cheeses, and meats. The adobe bins in the *granero* were full of grain to be ground into flour. Josefina and her sisters had made strings of squash slices, apple slices, red chiles, and herbs. The strings would hang near the hearth where they would dry and be handy for use in cooking throughout the winter. Josefina always enjoyed the cheerful bustle in the kitchen at harvest time, but it was a treat to be out and away today, high up on this golden hillside with her sisters.

The morning had flown by. Now it was mid-day and the sisters gathered around the food Carmen had packed for them. Miguel found a sunny spot nearby and took his afternoon rest while the girls ate.

Josefina bit into a plum that was warm from the
sunshine. The breeze lifted her hair off her back and
cooled her face. "I wish Tía Dolores had been able
to come with us today," she said. "She'd enjoy this."
Tía Dolores had gone to the village. She was bringing
food to some of the villagers who had lost their crops
in the flood.

"Sí!" agreed Ana and Clara. Francisca had a mouthful of tortilla.

Josefina grinned. She took a sprig of rabbit brush
out of her basket and pretended to be Tía Dolores.
"We'll put these flowers to good use, won't we, girls?"
she said, imitating Tía Dolores's energetic manner. Ana
and Clara laughed, especially when Josefina put the
flowers to good use tickling them!

But Francisca grabbed the flowers away. "Whenever
Tía Dolores talks about putting things to good use, it
always ends up meaning more work for us," she grumbled. "All this weaving, for example."

Josefina smiled. "I *like* the weaving," she said.

"Well," said Francisca. "It's new to you. But I find
it very dull." She collapsed back on the grass and

fanned herself with the sprig of flowers. "I'm worn out from it!"

"Now, Francisca," Ana scolded in her kindly, motherly way. "You have plenty of energy for things you enjoy, like dancing. Pretend you're dancing while you work at the loom. Dance on the treadles!"

"I can't dance very well with the loom!" said Francisca shortly.

"You don't weave very well with the loom, either," said Clara. "Weaving is just the sort of slow, patient work you're not good at, Francisca."

Francisca made a face. "Work!" she said. "I thought that when Tía Dolores came, there would be *less* work for us, not *more*."

"She doesn't ask us to do any more than she does herself," said Clara.

"You're right," said Francisca, sitting up. "Tía Dolores is always at work. She's always trying to fix things and improve things and change things— especially *us*!" Francisca poked and prodded Clara's arm with the sprig of rabbit brush as she continued to complain. "Tía Dolores is always trying to poke and prod us into being different than we are. She's never satisfied. She always thinks we can be better."

"Tía Dolores came to teach us," said Ana. "She's not a servant."

"She certainly is not," agreed Francisca. "She seems to think she is the *patrona*! Look at how she's put herself in charge of the weaving business." Tía Dolores had also taken on the responsibility of keeping track of the number of blankets the rancho was producing.

"As Papá said, we must replace the sheep," Ana said calmly. She collected the remains of the food, and the girls started back down the hill with Miguel. Ana walked next to Francisca. "We should be grateful to Tía Dolores for her good idea and her hard work. She is helping us, and that is *exactly* what we asked her to do."

Francisca frowned. "Tía Dolores's help is not *exactly* what I expected it to be," she said. "Tía Dolores isn't, either. She seems different than she was when she came here the first time."

"Yes!" said Josefina. She turned around and walked backwards a few steps so that she could face her sisters. "Tía Dolores seems happier."

"I think she is," said Ana. "She even looks happier,

and prettier, too. She's not so thin and pale as she was."

"She's letting her skin get rough and red," said Francisca, who was vain about her own complexion.

Josefina did not like to hear Francisca criticize Tía Dolores. "Why are you speaking this way about Tía Dolores?" she asked Francisca. "You were the one who used to say that she was elegant and that her clothes were beautiful."

"She never wears those beautiful clothes anymore," said Francisca, "just everyday work clothes." She shook her head and said mournfully, "Soon, I expect none of us will have anything *but* worn-out, workaday clothes."

Clara snorted. "You'd have a fancy new dress if you'd ever settle down and finish it!" she said.

Francisca ignored her. "Tía Dolores is determined to weave all our wool into blankets," she said. "I'm sure she won't spare even enough for new sashes for us. Not that it matters how we look. We don't have time to do anything but work these days! We're up long before dawn—"

"Ah, that's it!" said Ana. "You are out of sorts because you have to get up so early!" Ana, Clara, and Josefina glanced at each other and hid their smiles.

Francisca was well known for being slow to rise in the morning. Ana went on, "Mamá always said no one has a sweeter temper than you do, Francisca—as long as you have plenty of sleep!"

Josefina noticed that when Ana mentioned Mamá, a strange look crossed Francisca's face. Francisca started to say something, but then she seemed to change her mind. She said nothing.

Josefina took hold of Francisca's hand and swung it as they walked together. "Remember the morning song Mamá used to sing to you to help you wake up?" she asked Francisca.

Ever so briefly, the strange look crossed Francisca's face again. Then she began to sing, "Arise in the morning . . ." She stopped. "How did it go?" she asked. "I've forgotten. Sing it for me, Josefina."

Josefina began to sing:

> *Here comes the dawn,*
> *now it gives us the light of day.*
> *Arise in the morning*
> *and see that day has dawned.*

Josefina sang the song in her clear, sweet voice as the girls made their way down the hill. Tía Dolores met them as they passed the orchard. She was carrying a basket full of apples, walking with her usual purposeful stride. Wisps of her ruddy auburn hair curled out from under her rebozo, and her skirt flapped in the wind.

"Josefina," she said, "I do love to hear you sing!" She smiled. "Perhaps you'll sing a special song for all the village to hear as part of the Christmas celebration this year."

Josefina could feel her own smile sink right off her face. "Oh, no, Tía Dolores!" she said quickly, too surprised to be polite. She spoke again, this time with more respect. "I mean, I beg your pardon, but no, thank you."

"Why not?" asked Tía Dolores. "A lovely voice like yours is a gift from God. I am sure God means you to use it to delight others, especially if you do so to celebrate Him."

Josefina thought of how it would feel to have everyone looking at her, everyone listening to her singing all alone. She shivered. It was scarier than lightning.

"I'm . . . sorry," she said, stumbling over the words.
"I just *couldn't.*"

Tía Dolores looked Josefina straight in the eye.
"You mean you don't *want* to," she said. "But perhaps
one day you will."

Josefina felt something jab her arm. It was the sprig
of rabbit brush, and Francisca was poking her with
it. Francisca raised one eyebrow and gave Josefina a
look that said, *You see? Remember what I said about Tía
Dolores poking and prodding us to be different than we are?
Wasn't I right?*

The First Love

A few nights later, Josefina sat on a stool close to the fire in the family sala. The evening air had a sharpness that warned of the wintry cold to come. Josefina curled up her toes inside her warm knitted socks. She and Clara were spinning wool into yarn. They were using long spindles called *malacates* to twist tufts of wool into one long strand of yarn as the wool spun around. Ana was putting her boys to bed. Francisca sat nearby sewing her fancy dress, which, as Clara had pointed out, she still had not finished.

Tía Dolores was at her writing desk, bent close to her work. *Scritch, scratch, scritch, scratch.* Josefina loved the sound Tía Dolores's quill pen made as she wrote in the ledger she used to keep track of the weaving business. Paper and ink were precious, so Tía Dolores made

her numbers small and filled every inch of every page.
Papá sat nearby at the table, quietly watching her write.

Josefina looked around the family sala. *A piano,
a writing desk, paper, pen, ink, and a ledger!* she thought.
*Tía Dolores has brought so many new things to this room,
Mamá wouldn't recognize it!* But Tía Dolores's things
were not the only changes. Papá looked different, too.
His face looked less tired, as if he were not so weighed
down with sorrow as he had been, and sometimes he
even whistled again, as he used to.

"There!" said Tía Dolores. She put her pen down
with a pleased expression. "Would you do me the
honor of looking at the figures?" she asked Papá.

"Sí," said Papá. Tía Dolores brought the ledger to
the table, and she and Papá looked at it together.

"This shows how many sacks of wool we have,"
explained Tía Dolores as she pointed to a column of
figures in the ledger. "And this shows how many blankets I think we can weave. And this shows how many
sheep we'll get when we trade the blankets."

Papá nodded. "Excellent," he said. "The weaving
business should do very well, God willing. I am grateful to you, Dolores."

"Your daughters have worked hard," she said.

"Sí," said Papá. "They weave. But you have taken care of all this." He patted the ledger. "It is fortunate that you can read and write."

"My aunt taught me when I lived with her in Mexico City," said Tía Dolores. She thought for a moment, and then she said, "And now, with your permission, I'll teach your daughters to read and write. Then they will be able to continue the weaving business after I have left."

Francisca gasped. Josefina knew that meant she was not happy at the thought of yet another new thing to do. Now they would have lessons in reading and writing on top of everything else!

Tía Dolores must have heard and understood the gasp, too, because she said, "The lessons won't add any time to the day. I have a little speller I brought with me from Mexico City. We'll use it when we sit by the fire at night. We will be putting our evenings to *very* good use."

Francisca spoke up boldly. "I don't see the need for learning to read and write," she said. "I have no time to read books, and no one ever sends letters that have anything to do with *me.*"

Tía Dolores smiled. "Ah, but soon they will, Francisca!" she said. "Soon your papá will be receiving letters from young men who want to marry you."

Francisca sniffed. "Hmph!" she said. "I won't read them! And I'll reply to any marriage proposal by handing the young man the squash."

"That's true," stated Clara. "She's already done it!" In fact, a young man had already proposed to Francisca. She had indeed followed the old custom of giving him a squash to let him know she was not interested in marrying him.

"Letters proposing marriage can be very persuasive," said Tía Dolores. "Your papá won your mamá's heart with his letters!"

Francisca's dark eyes were flinty. "Mamá could not read," she said.

"No," said Tía Dolores. "But she always said that she loved the way your papá signed his name with such fancy flourishes."

Papá laughed. "I was young and foolish," he said. "It was the custom to make flourishes to show what an important person you were, and to make your

signature different from anyone else's. I don't bother
with flourishes anymore."

"Please won't you show us how you used to do it,
Papá?" asked Josefina.

Papá smiled but shook his head. "No, no. It's a
waste of paper," he said.

"Not at all," said Tía Dolores. She handed him the
pen and the green glass inkwell.

"Very well," said Papá agreeably. Josefina stood
next to him and Clara peered over his shoulder. As
they watched, Papá wrote his name in handsome,
upright letters. Then, under his name, Papá made
graceful swirls and curving spirals that looked like a
long, lovely curl of ribbon.

"Oh, Papá, it's beautiful!" said Josefina. She turned
to Tía Dolores. "Will we really learn to write like that?"
she asked.

"Sí!" said Tía Dolores. "We'll begin tomorrow."

Josefina stared at Papá's beautiful writing. Then she
looked up to smile at Francisca. Surely Francisca would
enjoy learning to do something as fancy and elegant-
looking as this!

But Francisca was gone. She had slipped out

quietly, without saying good night or waiting for Papá's blessing.

✹

Something woke Josefina in the middle of the night. It was a sound, just a small sound, but one that made Josefina sit up and tilt her head and listen hard. As her eyes adjusted to the darkness, Josefina saw that Francisca was not in her bed. Quietly, so as not to wake Clara, Josefina pulled on her moccasins and wrapped herself in her blanket. She crept outside. Francisca was sitting in the courtyard. She was wrapped in her blanket, too. There was no moon, but the stars were so big and bright Josefina could see Francisca's face. It was streaked with tears.

Josefina was surprised. She had not seen Francisca cry since Mamá died. "Francisca!" Josefina whispered as she came near. "What's the matter?"

"Go away," said Francisca fiercely.

Josefina knelt down next to her sister. "Are you hurt?" she asked. "Are you ill? Shall I fetch Tía Dolores?"

"No!" said Francisca. She spoke with such force

Josefina was startled. Her voice sounded hard as she said, "I've had quite enough of Tía Dolores!"

"What do you mean?" asked Josefina.

Francisca wiped the tears off her cheeks with an impatient hand. "Don't you see what's happening?" she asked. "Has Tía Dolores's praise for your sewing and weaving made you blind? Has she made you feel like such an important person that you don't care how she's changing everything? Nothing is the same as it was when Mamá was alive." Suddenly the bitterness left Francisca's voice. It was replaced by sadness. "Every change makes Mamá seem farther and farther away," she said. "Every change makes me feel as if I'm losing Mamá again. And oh, Josefina! I miss Mamá so!"

"So do I," said Josefina passionately. Her heart ached with sympathy for Francisca. Now she saw why Francisca had complained about Tía Dolores. Josefina tried to make Francisca feel better. "I miss Mamá, too," she said. "But Tía Dolores is good and kind! She is only trying to help us."

"By changing us!" said Francisca. "Now she's going to make us learn to read and write. Mamá didn't read or write. Mamá didn't ask anyone to teach us to read or write. Reading and writing will be one more way Tía Dolores will pull us away from Mamá. It'll be just one more way she'll fill our heads and our hearts so that we'll have no room left for Mamá. We'll start to forget her. We've already started."

"Oh, Francisca!" said Josefina. "That's not true!" But a dark fear stole into Josefina's mind. Was Francisca right? It was true that Tía Dolores had changed their lives. Josefina herself had changed. Hadn't she braved the lightning? Hadn't she learned to weave? But did Tía Dolores's new ideas and new ways mean there was no room for the old ways? Was Tía Dolores making them forget Mamá?

Francisca straightened her shoulders. "I am not going to do it," she said firmly. "I won't learn to read and write." She stood up and looked down at Josefina. "You'll have to make your own choice," she said. "Decide for yourself." Then she left.

Josefina stayed alone in the courtyard. She looked up at the huge, endless black sky and felt as if she were adrift in it. The stars seemed to be all around her— above her and below her and surrounding her on every side. Josefina felt lost. Francisca made it sound as if learning to read would be disloyal to Mamá. She made it seem as if Josefina had to choose between Mamá and Tía Dolores, between the old and the new.

What should I do, Mamá? Josefina asked. But she knew there would be no answer. The stars were as silent as stones.

✿

Usually Josefina skipped and sang all the way to the stream on laundry day. But today she walked joylessly, thinking about the conversation she'd had with Francisca the night before.

Tía Dolores was waiting for Josefina by the stream. "There you are, Josefina!" she said cheerfully. "You're as quiet as a little shadow this morning. And where are your sisters?"

"They're helping Carmen in the kitchen," Josefina answered.

"Good!" said Tía Dolores. "Then after we do the laundry, you will have your first reading lesson by yourself!"

Josefina tried to smile.

If Tía Dolores noticed that Josefina was not paying much attention to the clothes she was washing, she was too kind to say anything about it. They worked in an unusual silence. Tía Dolores spread a freshly washed white cloth on a bush to dry. There were already three other white cloths on the bush. "Look, Josefina!" said Tía Dolores with laughter in her voice. "They're four white doves perched on a rosemary bush!"

Josefina's face lit up for the first time that day. "Oh!" she said. "Mamá used to say that poem sometimes!" She tried to recite the whole poem. "'Behold four little white doves, perched on a rosemary bush. They were . . . they were . . .'" Josefina faltered. "I can't remember the rest," she said sadly.

Tía Dolores nodded. "Don't let it trouble you," she said. She draped another cloth on the bush.

Josefina sighed so deeply and so unhappily that Tía Dolores gave her a questioning look. "Oh, Tía Dolores," Josefina said, full of misery. "It *does* worry me. I can keep things that remind me of Mamá in my memory box, but I can't keep her words anywhere, and I'm beginning to forget them. It makes me afraid that I'm beginning to forget Mamá herself."

Tía Dolores's eyes were gentle as she listened. When Josefina stopped talking, Tía Dolores dried her hands on her skirt and said, "Come with me, Josefina."

Josefina almost had to run to keep up with Tía Dolores's long strides. Tía Dolores led Josefina back to the house and into the family sala. Her writing desk was still there on its stand. Without saying a word, Tía Dolores opened the lid of the writing desk and pulled out a drawer. From a secret compartment in the drawer she took a little book bound in soft brown leather. She handed it to Josefina.

Very, very carefully, Josefina turned the pages of the book. She couldn't read the words, but on many pages there were little sketches. Josefina stopped when she came to a drawing of four white birds perched on a bush.

Tía Dolores read the words on the page aloud:

> *Behold four little white doves*
> *perched on a rosemary bush.*
> *They were saying to each other,*
> *"There's no love like the first love."*

As she listened, Josefina remembered hearing Mamá's own dear voice, low and lilting and full of love, saying those very words.

"Your mamá didn't read or write," said Tía Dolores. "She learned this poem by hearing our papá read it aloud to us when we were little girls. When I was in Mexico City, I made this book. In it I wrote prayers, poems, songs, stories, even funny sayings your mamá and I both loved when we were girls. It helped me feel close to her, even though I was far away." She smiled at Josefina. "When you learn to read and write, you can look in this book any time you like and read your mamá's words. In it you can write things you remember her saying. This book will be a place to keep her words safe, so that you'll never lose them."

Josefina smiled with tremendous relief and gladness. She felt as if she had received an answer from Mamá herself about what she should do. It was as if Mamá were encouraging her to learn to read and write. Francisca was wrong. Reading and writing wouldn't pull them away from Mamá—it would help them remember her. "Oh, please will you teach me to read this book?" Josefina asked Tía Dolores.

"This book and any other you like!" said Tía Dolores. "Reading is a way to hold on to the past, to travel to places you've never been, and to learn about worlds beyond your own time or experience. You'll find there are many grander books than this one! Would you like to keep this little book with your memory box to be your very own?"

"No, gracias," said Josefina. She smiled a little smile. "That wouldn't be putting it to good use! I think you ought to keep it and read to all of us from it sometimes."

"Very well," said Tía Dolores.

"But may I borrow it for a moment?" Josefina asked. "I'll be careful."

"Sí, of course!" said Tía Dolores.

"Gracias!" said Josefina.

With a light heart and light feet, Josefina ran to find Francisca. She was sweeping in the kitchen.

"Look, Francisca!" said Josefina breathlessly. She opened Tía Dolores's little book to the drawing of the four doves. "The words on this page are Mamá's poem about the four doves," she said. "Do you remember it?"

Francisca thought. "Just the last line," she said.

"I think it ends, 'There's no love like the first love.'"

"Sí!" said Josefina. "This whole book is filled with
prayers and poems and sayings of Mamá's. Tía Dolores
made it. Don't you see, Francisca? When we can read
this book, it will be like hearing Mamá's voice. And
when we can write, we can add things we remember
her saying. This book will be a place to keep her words
safe forever." Josefina put the book into Francisca's
hands.

Francisca looked at the book and smiled. She didn't
say anything, but her eyes were shining.

Josefina smiled back. "Come with me," she said.
"Perhaps Tía Dolores will read more to us."

The two sisters hurried to the family sala. "Tía
Dolores," said Josefina. "Francisca would like to hear
you read something of Mamá's from your book. Would
you read to us?"

"With pleasure," answered Tía Dolores. "But first,
I would like to write your names in the book."

Francisca and Josefina watched eagerly while Tía
Dolores dipped her pen in the ink. "This is your name,
Francisca," she said.

Scritch, scratch, the pen moved across the page in the

small book. "And now I'll write your name, Josefina."

"Be sure to add lots of flourishes," said Francisca, "to show what an important person she is!"

"I will!" said Tía Dolores. She wrote:

Maria Josefina Montoya

Christmas
Is Coming

he wind was playing with Josefina. First it
made her skirt billow out behind her and the
ends of her rebozo fly up like wings. Then it
swirled around and pushed against her back, hurrying
her along like a helpful but impatient hand. Josefina
smiled. She could see that the wind was playing with
her sisters and Tía Dolores, too. They looked like birds
with ruffled feathers as they were blown along the road
on this blustery morning.

Josefina, her three sisters, and Tía Dolores were on
their way to the village about a mile from their rancho.
The road ran between the stream and the fields and
under tall cottonwood trees. The trees were bare now.
The windswept fields were a wintry, stubbly brown.
It was December. Christmas was coming, and today
everyone was gathering to clean the church so that it

would be ready to decorate. Josefina's papá had gone ahead with a burro loaded with wood for Christmas bonfires. The sisters and Tía Dolores would join him and their friends and neighbors at the church.

"Oh!" exclaimed Francisca, exasperated. The wind was blowing her hair so that it curled wildly around her face. Francisca was always careful about how she looked, especially when she was going to the village. She pulled her rebozo up over her head and tried to hold it in place with one hand as she struggled to carry a basket in her other hand.

Josefina didn't care if her hair was windblown. She slipped her arm under Francisca's basket. "I'll carry this," she said.

"Gracias," said Francisca. She let go of the basket and held her rebozo tightly under her chin with both hands.

Josefina glanced at the bright red chiles in the basket. "Why are you bringing these?" she asked Francisca.

"They're for Señora Sánchez," said Francisca.

"Don't you remember, Josefina?" asked Ana. "Mamá always gave Señora Sánchez some of our chiles at this time of year. Señora Sánchez claimed she couldn't make her traditional stew without them."

"Oh, that's right," said Josefina. "I remember."

Tía Dolores smiled at Josefina. "I'm eager to taste Señora Sánchez's famous stew," she said. "I'm glad Christmas is coming soon."

Josefina could only manage a very small smile in return. She saw that Clara was frowning. Ana and Francisca didn't look very enthusiastic, either.

Tía Dolores looked at the sisters' faces. "What's the matter?" she asked.

Ana answered. "When Mamá was alive, Christmas was always happy," she said. "But last Christmas was the first one after Mamá died. All we could think of was how much we missed her."

Tía Dolores spoke quietly. "It must have been very hard," she said.

Josefina slid her hand into Tía Dolores's. She knew that last Christmas must have been hard for her, too. Tía Dolores had been far away in Mexico City when Mamá, her sister, died. How sad and lonely she must have been!

"Last year, Christmas was very quiet," said

Francisca. "There were no parties or dances, out of respect for Mamá. No one felt like celebrating anyway."

For a while the sisters and Tía Dolores walked without talking. They were all remembering last year and wondering what this Christmas would be like. Josefina listened to the stream as it splashed over rocks and around curves. The stream flowed steadily and cheerfully. Josefina wished she could be as carefree about the holiday that lay ahead.

She asked Tía Dolores about one thing that was worrying her. "Would it be wrong to be happy this Christmas?" she asked. "Would it be disrespectful to Mamá?"

"No, I don't think so," said Tía Dolores. "The time of mourning has passed. Christmas is a blessed time. I'm sure God means for us to be happy, and to celebrate the birth of His son, Jesús." She looked down at Josefina. "And I'm sure your mamá would want you to be happy. She'd want you to pray and sing and celebrate with your friends and neighbors."

"Sí," Ana agreed. "Mamá would want us to follow all the Christmas traditions."

"I think so, too," said Francisca.

"Well," Clara said flatly. "We may follow the traditions, but they won't be the same without Mamá."

Somewhere inside Josefina a knot tightened. *Clara is right*, she thought.

"Mamá loved Christmas traditions," Josefina said to Tía Dolores. "She even started a new one in our family. Every Christmas, she'd make a doll dress for—"

"Oh, Josefina!" exclaimed Ana, interrupting. "You're talking about Niña, aren't you? Niña should have been given to you last Christmas."

"But she never was," said Josefina.

Tía Dolores looked puzzled. "Who's Niña?" she asked.

Ana explained, "When I was eight, Mamá made a doll for me. She named the doll Niña. Every Christmas, Mamá made a new dress for Niña. Then, the year Francisca was eight, I gave Niña to her."

"Sí," said Francisca. "And the Christmas when Clara was eight, I gave Niña to *her*."

"Of course, last year Mamá was not here to make a dress for Niña," said Ana sadly. She turned to Clara.

"But you could have given Niña to Josefina anyway, Clara. What happened?"

Josefina was curious to hear Clara's answer.

But Clara only shrugged and said, "I guess I forgot."

"Never mind, Clara," said Tía Dolores. "You can give the doll to Josefina this Christmas. I'll help you make a new dress for her. Where is Niña? I've never seen her."

"I haven't seen her in a long time, either," said Francisca.

"Neither have I," said Josefina, looking at Clara.

"Oh, she's around somewhere," said Clara. Her voice sounded unworried, but just for a second, a troubled look clouded her eyes. The look came and went so quickly, Josefina thought she must have imagined it.

Francisca, who was messy, liked to tease Clara, who was neat. "Heavens!" she said. "Do you mean to say that you've *lost* Niña?"

"She's not lost," said Clara crossly, kicking a pebble with her shoe. "I told you. She's around somewhere. I'll look for her when I have time."

"Would you like me to help you look?" Josefina

asked. She didn't want to make Clara more cross, but she really did want Niña. "Christmas is coming soon, and—"

"I know!" said Clara sharply. "I don't need any help! I'll find her!"

"Of course you will, Clara," said Tía Dolores.

Tía Dolores sounded so sure that Clara would find Niña. Josefina wished *she* could be as sure. How could Clara possibly have misplaced something as precious as Niña? Where could the doll be?

At that moment, Josefina made up her mind. She was going to look for Niña herself, no matter what Clara said. After all, Niña was *supposed* to be hers. Josefina's decision to look for Niña cheered her. She couldn't help feeling a little hopeful, just as she couldn't help feeling a little excited because she heard music. Josefina quickened her steps. The music was faint but clear, floating up from the village.

"Listen!" said Tía Dolores.

They all lifted their faces and listened. The music grew louder and stronger. It seemed to urge them, *Come along! Come along!* Soon they were all walking so fast they were practically dancing. Josefina's thick

braid bounced against her back, and even sensible
Clara skipped a little bit. The sound of the music
mixed in the air with the spicy scent of burning
piñón wood. As they came to the village, they saw
smoke rising up from chimneys into the cloudless
blue sky.

It was a small village. Josefina knew everyone in
all of the twelve families who lived there. She knew
their houses, too, which were built close together and
seemed to lean toward each other like old friends. The
houses were made of earth-colored adobe. They were
surrounded by hard-packed dirt, fenced pens for the
animals, and vegetable gardens now sleeping under
bumpy winter blankets of brown dirt. Most of the
houses faced the clean-swept *plaza* at the center of the
village. The biggest and most important building in
the village was the church. It was one story tall except
for the front, where the bell was hung high above
the doors.

Today, the doors of the church were wide open.
People scurried in and out carrying brooms and
brushes, tools, and scrubbing rags. They hauled big,
sloshing tubs of water up from the stream.

"Buenos días! It's good to see you! How are you today?" everyone called out when they saw Tía Dolores and the sisters.

"Buenos días! We're very well, thank you," they called back over the sound of the music and the noise of dogs barking and hammers pounding. People were talking, and every once in a while Josefina would hear swoops of laughter from the little children as they chased one another.

Clara, Francisca, and Ana went inside the church to start working. But Tía Dolores and Josefina lingered outside next to the musicians. One man was playing a guitar, and two others were playing violins. As Josefina and Tía Dolores listened, the music changed. The men began to play a slow, sweet song. All the noise and conversation seemed to fade away for Josefina. All she could hear was the music.

"I haven't heard this lullaby since I was a child," said Tía Dolores. She hummed along with the music for a moment, and then she asked Josefina, "Please, will you sing it for me?"

Josefina nodded. Very softly, she began to sing:

Sleep, my beautiful baby,
Sleep, my grain of gold.
The night is very cold,
The night is . . .

Josefina's throat tightened, and she couldn't finish the song. She turned her head away and looked down at the basket of chiles she was carrying so that Tía Dolores wouldn't see that her eyes had filled with tears.

But Tía Dolores had seen them already. She put her hand under Josefina's chin and gently turned Josefina's face toward her.

"Mamá used to sing that lullaby to me when I was little," said Josefina. "Papá played it on his violin. And we always sang it together at church on Christmas Eve to baby Jesús."

Tía Dolores used the soft edge of her sleeve to dry Josefina's cheek. Then she asked, "Does everyone sing it?"

"Everyone sings the end," said Josefina. "But not the first part. That's sung alone by the girl who is María in *Las Posadas*."

"You know," said Tía Dolores. "You're old enough
to be María."

"Oh, I couldn't!" said Josefina. Her heart pounded
faster at the very thought! Las Posadas was one of
the most important and holy Christmas traditions.
For nine nights in a row, everyone in the village acted
out the story of the first Christmas Eve, when María
and José were searching for shelter before baby Jesús
was born. A girl took the role of María, riding a burro
just as Jesús's mother did, and a man took the role of
José. María and José and their followers went from
house to house asking for shelter. Again and again
they were turned away, until finally they were welcomed into the last house. On Christmas Eve, the
final night of Las Posadas, everyone was welcomed
into the church instead of a house, and then Midnight
Mass began.

"Sometimes," said Tía Dolores thoughtfully, "a girl
wants to be María because she wants to pray for something special. I wonder what your prayer would be,
Josefina, if you were María?"

Josefina did not have to wonder. She knew what
her prayer would be. "I'd pray that this will be a happy

Christmas," said Josefina, "for us and for Mamá in heaven."

Tía Dolores smiled. "That's a good prayer," she said. "Are you sure you don't want to be María?"

Josefina listened to the last notes of the lullaby. Part of her wanted to be María, but part of her knew she couldn't do it. "Last year, I could hardly sing the songs in Las Posadas," she said. "They made me so sad, because they reminded me that Mamá was gone. I'm afraid it'll be the same this year." She shook her head. "I couldn't possibly be María."

"I understand," said Tía Dolores. "It's still too soon for you." She tucked a strand of Josefina's hair behind her ear. "Let's go in now."

Josefina nodded, and walked into the church with Tía Dolores.

The church was usually a quiet, solemn place, and dim because the windows were very small and set deep in the thick walls. But today it was busy and noisy. Light poured in from the open doors and peeked through gaps in the roof where it had been damaged in a storm that fall.

Everywhere Josefina looked, she saw friends and

neighbors and workers from Papá's rancho who'd put
aside their usual chores to come and clean the church.
Señora Sánchez, Señora López, and several other
women chatted together as they swept. Josefina saw
Papá's sister, Tía Magdalena, with a group of women
who were polishing candlesticks. Ana, Francisca,
and Clara were in a group of girls who were dusting.
Boys, who were supposed to be scattering water over
the floor to settle the dust, were splashing each other.
Most of the men of the village stood together, their
arms crossed over their chests, looking up at the roof
and discussing the damage caused by the storm in
the fall.

Josefina saw Papá standing with the men. Then
Papá excused himself. "There you are!" he said to
Josefina and Tía Dolores. "I was looking for you."

"We stopped outside to listen to the music," Tía
Dolores explained.

"I might have known!" Papá said. His eyes twin-
kled. "You two are the musicians in our family."

Josefina could tell that Papá's compliment pleased
Tía Dolores because she blushed a little. "Well," she
said, "we're ready to work now!"

"Good," said Papá. He caught the eye of Señor García, who came over.

Señor García was the *mayordomo*. It was his job to assign tasks, because he and his wife took care of the church. Señor García was an old man, thin and stooped, with very white hair. He had a husky voice and stately manners. Everyone respected him for his knowledge and liked him for his kindness.

"God bless you!" Señor García said to Tía Dolores and Josefina. "I'm glad to see you. We need good willing hands like yours to help! I'm afraid the storm has made our work harder than usual. The roof caused terrible damage when it fell in. We have a lot to do before the priest comes on Christmas Eve. Will you two help with the sweeping?"

"We'd be glad to," said Tía Dolores.

"Gracias," said Señor García. Then he turned to Papá. "May I ask your family to wash and iron the altar cloth, as you have done for many years?"

"Of course," said Papá.

"I remember when your dear wife gave that cloth to the church," said Señor García. "She'll be in our prayers this Christmas, I'm sure."

"Sí," said Papá quietly.

Señor García turned to Josefina again. "Josefina," he said. "I was wondering if you would like to be María in Las Posadas this Christmas, perhaps to offer a special prayer for your mamá?"

Josefina froze. Papá looked at her, waiting to hear her answer.

Tía Dolores put her arm around Josefina's shoulders. "It's very kind of you to ask, Señor García," she said. "But I think not this year."

"Ah, I see, I see," said Señor García gently. "Perhaps next year . . . Well, well, Margarita Sánchez can be María this Christmas."

Josefina didn't say anything. Just for a moment she leaned into Tía Dolores's arm, grateful for her understanding. Then she went to find Señora Sánchez to give her the basket of chiles.

✹

The morning flew by so fast that Josefina was surprised when Señor García called everyone together for the closing prayer. "May God accept our work here today as a prayer of thanks for His merciful love," he said.

"Amen," said everyone together.

Josefina said her good-byes and walked out into the sunshine with her family. She had enjoyed sweeping and listening to the singsong of the women's voices as they gossiped and chattered around her. It had been nice to be part of the friendly group all scrubbing and sweeping and dusting together. Because of their work, the church shone. But now Josefina headed home with eager steps. She was determined to begin looking for Niña that very afternoon.

Where Is Niña?

CHAPTER 10

osefina closed her eyes and tried to picture Niña. The last time Josefina had seen her, Niña was wearing a pale blue skirt. Her arms and legs were flat because some of her stuffing had fallen out, and her black yarn hair was tangled. Josefina clearly remembered Niña's lively black eyes and smiling pink mouth, and she was pretty sure she remembered a green sash tied around Niña's waist. *I'll just keep my eyes sharp for any bit of green or black or pale blue*, Josefina thought. *Niña has to be somewhere.*

The first place Josefina looked was in the room she shared with Clara and Francisca. Standing on tiptoe, Josefina ran her hand along all the high shelves built into the walls. She looked in corners, under blankets, and behind the trunk that Clara and Francisca kept their clothes in. No Niña.

Josefina opened the trunk to search inside. Clara's clothes were folded neatly and stacked in precise piles. Josefina looked between them and under them but saw nothing. Francisca's clothes were loosely folded and piled in the trunk in such a haphazard way that Josefina had to dig through them. She did find a missing stocking, a broken button, and a hair ribbon that Francisca had loudly complained about losing. But she didn't find Niña.

Josefina sat back on her heels and sighed. *Where is Niña?* she wondered.

It was a question she asked herself hundreds of times a day as Christmas came nearer. No matter where she was or what else she was doing, Josefina was looking for Niña. She'd start searching early in the morning when the snow on the mountains still had its cool blue glow, and she wouldn't stop until late in the afternoon when sunset made the snow look rosy.

Josefina's eyes searched the sala when she knelt there first thing in the morning for prayers with her family. Every time she walked to the stream to fetch water for the day, she looked around, hoping to see Niña hiding behind a rock or nestled at the foot of a

tree. She explored every nook and cranny of the storerooms, the stables, and the chicken coops as she did her
daily chores. She looked in the kitchen while she made
bizcochito cookies and in the courtyard while she waited
for bread to bake. She looked in the cradle when she
rocked Ana's baby son, Antonio, to sleep. She looked
in the weaving room behind the looms, in the stacks of
finished blankets, and in baskets full of wool waiting to
be carded and spun. Still no Niña.

In desperation, Josefina even searched the goats'
pen. "You haven't eaten Niña, have you?" she asked her
old enemy, Florecita. The yellow-eyed goat looked at
Josefina, blinked once, and turned away.

Josefina tried hard not to be discouraged, even
though she soon felt as if she'd searched every inch
of the rancho. Then one day, Josefina and her sisters
and Tía Dolores were invited to Señora Sánchez's
house. Josefina was glad to go. She knew that Clara
and Margarita Sánchez used to play dolls together.
Maybe *that's* where Niña was. At least it was a new
place to look!

✿

"Buenos días! Please come in!" said Señora Sánchez
as she welcomed everyone to her house. Almost all of
the women and children from the village were there.
The women had brought with them scraps of cloth and
paper. They were using them to make flowers called
ramilletes to decorate the church on Christmas Eve. Tía
Dolores had brought some yellow material that was left
over from the new dress Josefina had made for herself.

Señora Sánchez was a stout, good-hearted woman
who was well known for being generous and neigh-
borly. She'd been a special friend of Mamá's. They
used to visit back and forth to share food and news
and advice. Señora Sánchez always had time to sit and
talk. And yet she seemed always to have something
delicious cooking on the hearth, and her house was as
neat as a pin. Mamá used to say she didn't know how
Señora Sánchez did it!

But Señora Sánchez's house wasn't neat today. The
women were gathered in the kitchen around the bright
jumble of colored scraps. Josefina searched the kitchen
with her eyes, hoping to see Niña. There was no doll to
be seen, but Josefina couldn't help smiling at the pile of
finished ramilletes. It looked as if a flower garden were

blooming right there in the middle of Señora Sánchez's kitchen! Josefina turned to Tía Dolores. "The ramilletes remind me of the flowers Mamá planted in our courtyard," she said.

"Josefina, your mamá would be pleased with the way you've cared for the flowers she planted," said Tía Magdalena, who was Josefina's godmother.

All the women murmured in agreement.

"Things grew well for your mamá," said Señora López.

"Of course they did!" said Señora Sánchez. "And no wonder! She used to say to me, 'You must treat flowers like people!'"

The women nodded, and Señor García's wife said, "Well, she certainly treated people kindly. Look how beautifully her daughters are growing." Señora García turned to Tía Dolores. "And you've done well to teach the girls to read and write, and to encourage them to weave."

Tía Dolores smiled. "They've worked very hard," she said.

Josefina felt a warmth that came from more than the fire and the hot, sweet mint tea Señora Sánchez served. She had known these women all her life, as far back as she could remember. They'd helped her when she was a fat-legged toddler always underfoot and falling down just like the toddlers there today. They'd known her when she tagged along watching Clara and Margarita play dolls, back before Niña disappeared. When Mamá died, all of these women had lost a dear friend. Josefina knew they'd never forget Mamá, any more than she herself would.

"Look!" said Francisca. She held a cloth flower behind one ear. It was made of the yellow material that Tía Dolores had brought. Francisca twitched her skirts and swirled around gracefully as if she were dancing.

Everyone laughed. Ana said, "The flower looks pretty in your hair, Francisca. But it'll look just as pretty in the church on Christmas Eve!"

"We'll put the ramilletes in an arch over the altar," said Señora García to the girls. "And we'll put the cloth your mamá made on the altar."

"Didn't she have a fine hand for *colcha* embroidery?" said Tía Magdalena. "No village in New Mexico has a lovelier Christmas altar cloth."

Señora Sánchez turned to her daughter Margarita, who was going to be María in Las Posadas this year. "Sing for us, Margarita," she said. "Sing the lullaby we always sing on Christmas Eve."

Josefina held her breath while Margarita sang:

> *Sleep, my beautiful baby,*
> *Sleep, my grain of gold.*

And everyone but Josefina joined in:

> *The night is very cold,*
> *The night is very cold.*

This time, the lullaby didn't make Josefina cry. Instead, as she listened, Josefina thought, *A song like this must go straight up to God like a prayer.*

With all her heart, Josefina wished she had the courage to be María in Las Posadas this Christmas. But with all her heart she was sure that she did not.

The December afternoon was short. The weak winter sun slid down behind the mountains early, and it was nearly dusk when Papá came to walk home with

Tía Dolores and the sisters. He had been to the church to get the trunk that had the Christmas altar cloth in it.

Señora Sánchez beckoned to Josefina. "Come with me," she said. "I have something for you and your sisters, to thank you for the chiles."

Josefina followed Señora Sánchez outside. She was very surprised when Señora Sánchez handed her a little cage made out of bent wood. Inside the cage there was the plumpest, prettiest black-and-white hen Josefina had ever seen. "Oh, Señora Sánchez!" Josefina exclaimed. "Gracias!"

Señora Sánchez beamed a generous smile. "She's a vain little hen, very proud of herself, I'm afraid!" she said. "But she has reason to be proud. She lays very fine eggs. I thought you and your sisters could raise her chicks to increase your flock. I know you'll take good care of her."

Josefina thanked Señora Sánchez again. She held up the cage to look at the hen, who puffed herself up and met Josefina's gaze with her beady black eyes. Then Papá strapped the hen's cage onto the burro, next to the trunk from the church. He and Tía Dolores and the sisters began the long walk home.

"Adiós!" the women called out after them. "God keep you well!"

Josefina turned and waved. "Adiós!" she called.

It had been a long, full day and Josefina was tired. As she walked along next to Clara she said happily, "The ramilletes we made will look beautiful in the church, won't they?"

"I suppose so," said Clara, rather sourly. "Of course, no one will know how to arrange them as nicely as Mamá used to." She sighed. "Oh, well, at least the altar cloth will look all right. *It* will be the way it used to be."

✸

When they were home at the rancho, Papá carried the trunk into the kitchen and set it down near the fire. "Wait till you see Mamá's altar cloth," Josefina said to Tía Dolores. "The birds that Mamá embroidered on it look so real you expect them to sing!"

Tía Dolores smiled. She knelt next to the trunk. Papá and all the sisters crowded around, peering over her shoulders as she lifted the lid. Tía Dolores lifted the altar cloth out of the trunk and they all looked at it. For a moment, no one said anything. Then Papá pulled his breath in sharply, as if something had hurt him. Without a word, he turned and left the room.

Josefina was confused. What was this torn, bedraggled cloth in Tía Dolores's hands? This cloth looked like a rag. It was chewed by mice. It smelled of mildew. It was water-stained and dirty. It couldn't be Mamá's beautiful embroidered altar cloth. But it was.

"Oh, no," said Ana, sounding miserable. "Water from the flood must have rotted the leather of the trunk so that mice and dampness got in. Just look at the damage that's been done."

"It's *ruined*!" Clara cried out. "It's ruined, just like Christmas!" She rushed from the room.

The door slammed behind her, and the whole room and everyone in it was shaken. It wasn't like Clara to act like that. Her words echoed in Josefina's head: *It's ruined, just like Christmas* . . . The knot inside Josefina tightened again. Just when Josefina had begun to hope that this Christmas might be happy, *this* had to happen. The beautiful altar cloth Mamá had made so lovingly was destroyed. It hurt Josefina to look at it on Tía Dolores's lap.

Tía Dolores unfolded the altar cloth slowly,

never minding the dirt and mildew that soiled her skirt. The more she unfolded it, the more damage Josefina saw.

Francisca lifted one corner, using just the tips of her fingers. "Just look!" she said. "It's in shreds!"

Ana sighed. "I'm glad Mamá is not here to see this," she said. "It would break her heart."

Tía Dolores didn't say anything. She examined the cloth carefully, running her hands over it. Then she said, "I think we can repair this."

Ana, Francisca, and Josefina looked at each other. "But how?" asked Francisca.

"First, we'll wash it," said Tía Dolores. "Then we'll iron it. We'll mend the embroidery wherever we can."

"But what about the embroidery that the mice chewed away?" asked Ana.

"We'll replace it with new embroidery," said Tía Dolores.

Francisca looked doubtful. "We'll need Clara for that," she said. "Mamá taught us all colcha embroidery, but Clara's the best. She's the only one who's even close to doing colcha as well as Mamá."

"Very well," said Tía Dolores. "Josefina, please

go to Clara and ask her to come back so that I may speak to her."

Josefina nodded. Quickly, she crossed the courtyard to the room she shared with Francisca and Clara. The door was partly open, and through it Josefina heard the sound of Clara crying. Josefina stood still, not sure what to do. As she hesitated, she looked into the room. It was dark, but Josefina saw Clara open the clothes trunk and take out an old skirt that was neatly folded into a thick bundle. Clara unfolded the skirt. Josefina saw a bit of something pale blue, a flash of green, *and there was Niña!*

Josefina gasped in surprise and bewilderment. Clara had Niña! The doll had been hidden in Clara's trunk all this time! Josefina took one step into the room, then stopped short when she saw Clara bury her face in Niña and sob. Clara cried as if her heart were broken, and she held on to Niña as if the doll were her only comfort in the world. Josefina turned away quietly so that Clara wouldn't hear her.

When Josefina got back to the kitchen, Ana and Francisca were gone. Tía Dolores was alone, still holding the altar cloth.

"Is Clara coming?" asked Tía Dolores.

"I . . . I don't know," stammered Josefina.

Tía Dolores looked confused. She asked, "Didn't you speak to her?"

"No," said Josefina. Suddenly, she burst out, "Tía Dolores, Clara has Niña! I saw her! The door was open a little and when I looked in, I saw Clara holding the doll!" Josefina spoke as if she could hardly believe what she had seen. "Clara has known where Niña is all along. She's been keeping her for herself!"

Tía Dolores put the altar cloth down and took both Josefina's hands in her own. "I'm not sure I understand it," she said slowly. "But I think Clara misses your mamá very, very much. Your mamá made Niña, and she made a new dress for her every Christmas. So Niña is a way for Clara to feel close to your mamá. She's a comfort. Clara needs her."

"But why did she pretend she didn't know where Niña was?" asked Josefina indignantly. "That wasn't *true*."

"Do you remember the other day when you told me how you're not ready to be María in Las Posadas?" Tía Dolores asked.

Josefina nodded.

"Well, Clara is not ready to give you Niña. That's why she's hiding her," said Tía Dolores. She looked at Josefina's long face and tried to cheer her. "At least we know that Niña isn't lost. She's safe. That's good, isn't it?"

"I guess so," Josefina admitted grudgingly. "But when will Clara give her to me? Will Niña ever be mine?"

Tía Dolores sighed. "I don't know," she said. "No one knows, probably not even Clara. It may take a long time." She put Josefina's hands aside and picked up the altar cloth again. "Just as it will take time to repair this altar cloth. But we'll do it. The sooner we begin, the better." Tía Dolores tried to tease a smile out of Josefina. "What do I always say?" she asked.

Josefina had to smile just a little bit, in spite of Clara, in spite of Niña, and in spite of herself. "You always say, 'The saints cry over lost time.'"

"Precisely!" said Tía Dolores briskly. "We'll start tomorrow!"

The Silver Thimble

nd they did start repairing the altar cloth the very next day—everyone except Clara. Josefina helped Tía Dolores wash the altar cloth in warm, soapy water and rinse it in clear, cool water. Gently, Tía Dolores wrung out the cloth. Then she and Josefina spread it to dry in a sunny corner of the back courtyard. When the cloth was dry, Ana ironed it smooth, being careful not to scorch it with the hot irons heated by the fire. Francisca helped Josefina mend some of the holes the mice had chewed, and Tía Dolores cut off the end where the holes were too big to mend. She attached a new piece of material in its place.

At last the time came to begin the colcha embroidery. Tía Dolores and the four sisters gathered in front of the fire as they did every evening. Tía Dolores spread out the altar cloth. "What shall we embroider?" she asked, looking at the sisters.

Josefina looked at the altar cloth. Firelight brightened the colors of the designs that Mamá had stitched. Josefina had an idea. "Wait," she said. Very quickly, she went to her room and found her memory box, the little box in which she kept things that reminded her of Mamá. She brought the box back to the fireside. "Mamá made the altar cloth," she said. "I think we should embroider things on it that she loved. Maybe the things in my box will give us ideas."

Josefina opened her memory box, and Francisca took a swallow's feather out of it. "Mamá loved swallows," Francisca said. "I'll embroider swallows and other birds on the altar cloth."

Ana took a bit of lavender-scented soap out of the box. She smelled it. "I'll stitch sprigs of lavender," she said. "Mamá loved its scent."

"And I'll embroider leaves and flowers," said Josefina as she took a dried primrose out of her memory box. "Because Mamá loved them."

"And what will you embroider, Clara?" Tía Dolores asked.

Clara was only halfway in the firelight. She looked at the altar cloth with critical eyes. "It doesn't matter," she said. "We can't make that cloth look right again without Mamá anyway."

"We can," said Tía Dolores firmly. "It'll take time, but we can repair it. And if we all work together, I think we'll even enjoy doing it."

Clara drew back out of the light, but Josefina saw her face. It looked as sad as it did in the moment Josefina had seen Clara holding Niña and crying. Suddenly, Josefina felt sorry for Clara. "Doing the colcha embroidery makes me miss Mamá, too, Clara," Josefina said. "It makes her seem very far away, doesn't it?"

Clara didn't answer.

"Perhaps this will help," said Tía Dolores. She reached in her pocket and took out a silver thimble. "Your mamá gave this to me a long time ago when we were girls. She was trying to teach me how to do colcha. I didn't like it because I kept pricking myself with the needle and it hurt. She gave me the thimble to protect my finger. Now all of you may use it to protect *your* fingers."

Clara leaned forward on her stool. She looked at
the thimble and then at Tía Dolores. "If Mamá gave
something like that to me, I'd keep it forever," she said.
"I wouldn't dream of giving it away!"

Just like Niña, thought Josefina with a heavy heart.

"But it makes me happy to share the thimble,"
said Tía Dolores. "When we use it, we'll think of your
mamá with every stitch we make. Perhaps it will make
her seem closer, not farther away."

"Oh, please, may I use it?" Josefina asked.

Tía Dolores handed the silver thimble to Josefina
and she put it on her finger. It looked shiny in the light
of the fire. As she began stitching, Josefina used the
thimble to help push the needle through the cloth. She
knew Clara was watching her. When Josefina started
to tie a knot at the end of the wool she was using, Clara
moved next to her.

"Don't," said Clara. "Have you forgotten? Mamá
said never to knot the wool. Use your second stitch to
hold your first stitch in place. Here, let me show you.
I'll stitch the stem of that flower for you."

Clara spread the cloth over her knees and took the
needle from Josefina. She began to stitch. Francisca

nudged Ana, and Ana raised her eyebrows at Josefina as if to say, *This is a surprise!*

Josefina took the thimble off her finger. "Use this," she said.

Clara stopped for a moment and looked at the thimble. Then, slowly, she took it from Josefina and slipped it on her own finger. "Gracias," she said, but so quietly only Josefina could hear her.

Josefina gave herself the job of untangling knots in the wool Tía Dolores was using. When she looked up a little while later, Josefina saw that Clara had finished stitching the stem and was embroidering a yellow blossom on the end of it. Josefina saw that Clara's stitches were smooth and sure and secure.

She also saw that Clara hadn't taken the silver thimble off her finger.

✸

On a still, cold evening a few days later, Tía Dolores and the sisters were working on the altar cloth in front of the fire. "Francisca," said Josefina. "That chicken you're stitching looks just like the pretty little hen that Señora Sánchez gave us."

Francisca groaned and pretended to be annoyed. "It's not supposed to be a chicken," she said. "It's supposed to be a sparrow!" She held the altar cloth up so that Tía Dolores, Ana, and Clara could see it, too. "What do you think?" she asked. "Can we pretend that it's a very fat sparrow?"

"One that clucks instead of singing?" teased Josefina.

They all laughed, and Clara said, "I can fix it for you. It just needs its feathers smoothed a bit."

"Gracias!" said Francisca. She let Clara take her needle with relief.

Ana had been wearing the silver thimble, but now she handed it to Clara. "You'll need this," she joked. "Francisca's chicken might peck at you!"

Tía Dolores was right, thought Josefina as they all laughed again. *We are enjoying working together to repair Mamá's altar cloth.*

"I remember when Mamá taught me to do colcha," said Clara. "She told me, 'You'll like colcha. You have hands that need to be busy.'" Tía Dolores and the sisters smiled at Clara's memory. Josefina watched Clara stitch and admired, as she always did, the way the silver thimble shone in the firelight.

The four sisters and Tía Dolores worked on the cloth almost every evening, and it was a time Josefina looked forward to. They took turns wearing the silver thimble. Francisca made a game out of it. She said that whoever wore the thimble had to share a memory about Mamá. Sometimes the memories would make Josefina sad. But sometimes they made her laugh because they reminded her of happy times. Just as the thimble protected Josefina and her sisters from the pain of being pricked by the needle, it seemed also to protect them from the pain that memories of Mamá used to bring.

Repairing the altar cloth was slow work. But as the days went by, stitch by stitch the cloth became beautiful again. And as the days went by, bit by bit Josefina began to feel better about all the things this Christmas might bring—even though she was now quite sure Niña was *not* going to be one of them.

✹

Before they knew it, Christmas was only nine days away, and it was time for Las Posadas to begin. On the first night of Las Posadas, it was snowing lightly when Josefina and her family walked to the village. Papá led the way, holding a lantern high to light the road. When they came into the plaza, Josefina could see hot orange sparks from the bonfires rising up to meet the cold white snowflakes. The biggest bonfire was in front of the church. Almost all their friends and neighbors and all the workers from Papá's rancho had gathered around it. Everyone greeted the Montoyas when they joined the circle, and their breath puffed clouds into the sharp air. As Josefina watched Margarita Sánchez climb onto the burro and settle her skirts around her, she thought Margarita would be a very fine María. Because it was the village tradition, Margarita's papá was being José. He led the burro to the first house and everyone followed. He knocked on the door, and they all sang:

In heaven's name, we ask for shelter.

And the people inside sang back:

This is not an inn! Be on your way!

At first, Josefina didn't even try to join the singing. She hung back, expecting to feel the same heavy, ice-cold weight of sorrow she'd felt last year. Back then, she had missed the sound of Mamá's voice so much that the music had been painful to hear. Papá must have felt the same way, because he gave away his violin. But tonight, the music wasn't painful. It sounded gentle and familiar. Josefina listened very hard. It seemed to her that the music helped her remember the sound of Mamá's voice, and so she was glad to hear it. Josefina looked at the faces that surrounded her. She saw Señor García's thin, kindly old face and Margarita Sánchez's young, round face. She saw Ana, Francisca, and Clara with snow-flakes clinging to their hair. She heard Papá's voice, so low she could feel it inside her, and Tía Dolores's voice, strong and clear. It was a comfort to be surrounded by these good people who had loved Mamá too. *Oh, Mamá,* Josefina thought. *We all miss you so much!* Somehow, the thought made missing Mamá easier to bear.

Josefina shivered. But it was the beautiful music that made her shiver, not cold or sorrow. As she listened, Josefina thought about how people had been singing these same songs at Las Posadas for hundreds of years.

They sang to honor God and to remember the first
Christmas when Jesús was born. Josefina thought
back to when Mamá taught *her* the songs so that she
could join in the tradition. She remembered all the
Christmases when she and Mamá had taken part in
Las Posadas together, and the memories were both sad
and sweet.

Tonight, the last house the procession went to was
the Sánchez family's house. This time, after the people
outside asked for shelter, the people inside opened the
door wide. Josefina saw Señora Sánchez's good-natured
face in the doorway and heard her sing louder than
anyone else:

Come in, weary travelers. You are welcome!

Josefina grinned. No one could doubt that Señora
Sánchez truly meant the welcoming words from her
heart! And Josefina meant it, too, when she and the
others sang their thanks in return:

God bless you for your kindness,
And may heaven fill you with peace and joy!

Then everyone crowded inside for prayers and more singing before the party began. In the Sánchez family's house, the air was spicy with the delicious aroma of meat pies and tamales and, of course, Señora Sánchez's famous stew. Josefina saw Clara and Margarita warming themselves by the fire. They were looking at the ramilletes, and Clara was holding up a scrap of yellow cloth as if she were planning to make more flowers. Her face looked happy and eager.

Josefina thought that Clara must be feeling the same way she was—as if a heavy burden had started to slip away.

La Noche Buena

very day was colder than the one before, and
Christmas Eve day was bone-chilling. The
sky was dark as stone from dawn till dusk,
and sleet fell without stopping. Josefina's hands were
stiff as she and Clara put the final stitches in the altar
cloth late that afternoon.

At last the cloth was finished. Tía Dolores held one
end and Ana held the other so that they could fold it
carefully. One of the flowers Clara had embroidered
ended up on top. Tía Dolores stroked the flower gently.
"Clara," she said. "You have your mamá's gift for
embroidery. Truly you do."

"I can't tell Clara's flowers from those Mamá made,"
agreed Ana.

A quick, pleased smile lit Clara's face. She took the
silver thimble off her finger and held it out to

Tía Dolores. "Thank you for sharing this with us," she said.

Tía Dolores didn't take the thimble. Instead she said, "Perhaps Josefina will let us keep it in her memory box. It'll be handy there."

"Sí," said Josefina. "Go ahead, Clara. You can put the thimble in the box. It's on the shelf in our room."

But Clara put the thimble in the palm of Josefina's hand and then curled Josefina's fingers around it so that it was held tight in her fist. "No," Clara said. "I think you should go and put it in your memory box, Josefina."

"Sí, put it safely away," said Tía Dolores. "And Clara, you'd better go, too. It's time for you girls to change your clothes." She smiled. "It's Christmas Eve!"

Josefina and Clara hurried across the courtyard to their room. Francisca, who shared the room with them, had finished dressing. She'd left a small candle in the room to give Clara and Josefina light to dress by. But as they came in, it seemed to Josefina that the room was illuminated by more than one single candle. Josefina smiled when she saw why. Someone had laid out Josefina's best black lace *mantilla*, her comb, and her new dress on top of the trunk. The pretty yellow dress brightened the whole room. Josefina walked toward it, then stopped, stared, and gasped in surprise. For there, sitting on top of her yellow dress, was Niña!

Josefina lifted Niña up. She saw that Niña's face looked just as she remembered it. The eyes Mamá had sewn out of black thread still looked lively, and the mouth Mamá had sewn out of pink thread still smiled sweetly. Niña's yarn hair was smooth and untangled. Her arms and legs were plump with new stuffing. Best of all, Niña had a new yellow dress that exactly matched Josefina's. It had a long skirt and long sleeves gathered in puffs up near the shoulders. Niña even had a tiny new mantilla like Josefina's, and pantalettes and a petticoat. Josefina hugged Niña and kissed her soft cheeks.

"She's yours," said Clara.

"Oh, Clara!" Josefina whispered. "Gracias!" She hugged Niña closer. "I thought she never would be."

"Why not?" asked Clara.

"I . . . I knew that you had her," Josefina admitted, "and I—"

"You knew?" interrupted Clara.

"Sí," answered Josefina.

"Why didn't you say anything?" Clara asked.

"Well," said Josefina, "Tía Dolores told me that you needed her."

Very slowly, Clara nodded. "I did need her," she said. "I thought she was all I had left from Mamá. But now I know that I have Mamá's gift for embroidery, and I'll never lose that."

Josefina touched the smooth ribbon around the high waist of Niña's dress. "Did you make this dress for Niña?" Josefina asked.

"Sí," said Clara. "I wanted to carry on the tradition that Mamá started."

Josefina smiled broadly at Clara. "Niña's dress is beautiful," she said. "I think maybe you have Mamá's gift for making doll dresses, too!"

Clara smiled back. Then she looked lovingly at Niña. "I went to Niña for comfort because I thought I had nowhere else to go," she said. "But now I know that there's comfort all around me if I need it."

"Sí," said Josefina. "I'm finding that out also." She opened her fist, and the silver thimble shone in the candlelight. "I'll put the thimble in my memory box so that we can share it," Josefina said to Clara. "And we'll share Niña, too. She'll sleep between us from now on."

✹

Christmas Eve was called *la Noche buena*—the good night. And this Christmas Eve felt like a very good night to Josefina. Niña was hers to love and care for at last. The weather was still sleety and cold, so Josefina wore a rebozo crisscrossed over her chest and tied behind her waist under the outer blanket she wore for warmth. She tucked Niña inside her rebozo and held her tight as she and her family walked to the village. It was later than usual, because tonight Las Posadas would end at the church and the priest, Padre Simón, would begin Mass at the stroke of midnight. After Mass, everyone would stream out of the church into the frosty blackness and wish each other *feliz Navidad*— happy Christmas. Then there was going to be a party at the Garcías' house. Josefina knew there would be music and dancing and a wonderful feast. Ana was bringing a silver tray piled high with sweet bizcochito cookies like Mamá used to make. Josefina hugged Niña in happy anticipation of it all.

A big bonfire glowed gold in the darkness in front of the church. Josefina was glad to see it. She was glad to go inside the church, too, where it was dry. Sleet had beaded her blanket as if it were covered with thousands of tiny pearls. Josefina took the blanket off and shook it just inside the door of the church. She checked to be sure that Niña was held safe in her rebozo, then hurried to catch up with Papá and Tía Dolores and her sisters. They were near the altar with Señor García and other friends and neighbors who had come to decorate the church.

Tía Dolores gave the altar cloth to Señor García.

"Gracias, gracias!" said Señor García to Tía Dolores and the sisters. "I am told that all of you had to work hard to repair this. God bless you!"

"Everyone is grateful," added Señora López. "Now our altar will be as beautiful as it has been in years past."

"Padre Simón is on his way," said Señor García. "Some men from the village have gone to greet him and lead him to the church. Perhaps we had better begin to decorate. Soon it will be time to start Las Posadas."

Only a few candles were lit. Most were being saved for when Padre Simón would say Mass. The church was shadowy, and Josefina felt as if she and the others who quietly set about decorating were preparing a lovely surprise. Josefina helped Papá and Señor López arrange pine branches around the little wooden stable that was part of the Nativity scene. The branches smelled fresh with the tang of mountain air. Then Josefina helped put the carved wooden figures from the Nativity scene in their places. She helped spread the cloth on the altar and smooth out any wrinkles. Ana and Francisca and a group of girls had just finished arranging the colorful ramilletes in an arch over the altar when Señora Sánchez hurried into the church. She looked distressed.

"Pardon me, Señor García," she said breathlessly. "I'm afraid I have bad news. My daughter Margarita is ill. She must have caught a cold from being outside on these bitter nights. She is too ill to be María tonight. She can't stir from her bed!"

"Poor Margarita!" said Señor García.

Everyone dropped what they were doing and gathered around Señora Sánchez and Señor García. They shook their heads and murmured, "Oh, the poor child! Bless her soul!"

Josefina's heart beat fast. She asked herself a question, and thought hard about the answer. Slipping one hand inside her rebozo so that it was touching Niña, Josefina used the other hand to tug gently on Señor García's sleeve.

Señor García turned to her. Josefina's voice was small but steady as she looked up at him and said, "Please, Señor García, may I be María?" Everyone looked at Josefina as she went on, "I'd like to pray that this will be a happy Christmas for us and for my mamá in heaven."

Señor García's thin old face was solemn. Slowly, he nodded. "Sí, my child," he said to Josefina. "You may be María."

Josefina turned to Papá. "Will you be José?" she asked him.

"I will," said Papá gravely. He didn't smile, but he looked at Josefina with pride and love.

Tía Dolores did, too.

✹

When it was time, Josefina handed Niña to Clara for safekeeping. "Please hold her for me," Josefina said. "Keep her warm."

Clara took the doll. "I will," she promised.

They all went outside. The wind was blowing hard, driving the sleet so that it stung Josefina's face. Papá lifted Josefina up onto the burro's back. She knew Señor Sánchez's burro was gentle. But still, she felt very high off the ground. Josefina was glad Papá would be walking at her side leading the burro. She took the reins and held on tight.

A gust of wind made the skirt of her dress flutter. Papá was wearing an extra blanket over his sarape. He took it off now and said, "You'd better wear this over your own blanket. It'll keep you warm."

"Gracias," said Josefina as Papá wrapped her in the blanket. It covered her from head to foot.

As the villagers gathered to begin the procession, many people stopped to speak to Papá and Josefina. Gently, they touched Papá's shoulder or Josefina's foot or the end of the blanket Papá had wrapped around her. "May God grant you a good and long life," they said.

Josefina tried to sit up as straight as she could on the burro's back. Then, with a slow *clop clop* of the burro's hooves on the frozen ground, they moved to the first house. Papá knocked on the door, and they all sang:

In heaven's name, we ask for shelter.

And the people inside sang back:

This is not an inn! Be on your way!

Josefina's voice was unsteady at first. She felt nervous and stiff because she was self-conscious. But, as they had on every other night, the lovely music and words soon made Josefina forget all about herself and her shyness. After a while, Josefina was singing the Las Posadas songs in a voice that was full of all the hope and happiness of Christmas.

Papá led the burro from house to house. At each house, he and Josefina and everyone with them sang, asking for shelter. And at each house, the people inside sang back, telling them to go away. Then everyone inside the house came out to join the group behind Papá. After the last house, Papá turned back to the church. By that time, everyone in the whole village and all the workers from the rancho were in the crowd. Josefina felt as if everyone she knew and loved in the world were there behind her.

When they got to the church, Papá knocked on the doors. *Boom! Boom! Boom!* The sound echoed inside. Then everyone sang:

> *María, Queen of Heaven, begs for shelter*
> *For just one night, kind sir!*

Padre Simón opened one of the church doors just a bit. He looked out and sang:

> *Come in, weary travelers. You are welcome!*

Then Padre Simón flung both doors open wide. Golden candlelight flooded out. The church bell rang. And everyone sang:

God bless you for your kindness,
And may heaven fill you with peace and joy!

Papá lifted Josefina down off the burro. She was glad for his strong arms, because her legs felt wobbly and numb from the cold. The big blanket Papá had wrapped around her was weighted down with a coating of sleet, but when she took it off, her own blanket underneath it was dry.

"Josefina," she heard someone whisper. It was Clara, who handed Niña to her. Josefina tucked Niña safe inside her rebozo again. Then Tía Dolores took Josefina by one hand and Papá took the other, and they walked into the church behind Padre Simón. Ana, Francisca, Clara, and everyone else followed.

Josefina could hardly breathe. The church was so beautiful, she felt as if she were walking into a dream. All the candles were lit. Their brightness made the candlesticks shine and the polished wood glow. The candles cast a warm light on the Nativity scene in its nest of pine branches and on the delicate ramilletes arched gracefully above the altar.

But to Josefina, the most beautiful thing by far

was Mamá's altar cloth. Perhaps it was because she knew and loved every stitch of it after working on it for so long with Tía Dolores and her sisters. In the wavering candlelight, the soft, flowing leaves and flowers seemed to be floating in a gentle breeze, and the colors were rich and true. Josefina looked at the newly embroidered flowers with pride. *Mamá would be pleased,* she thought.

By now the church was full of people, and Padre Simón began the Mass. When it was time for her to sing the beginning of the lullaby, Josefina stood up, closed her eyes, and sang:

> *Sleep, my beautiful baby,*
> *Sleep, my grain of gold.*

Her voice was the only sound in the church, like a bird singing all alone on a mountaintop. Then Josefina opened her eyes, and everyone sang with her:

> *The night is very cold,*
> *The night is very cold.*

Josefina listened to all the voices soaring up around her, and she felt as safe and as loved as she used to feel when Mamá sang the lullaby to her.

Josefina hugged Niña close, sure that her prayer for a happy Christmas had been answered.

INSIDE Josefina's World

Today, New Mexico is part of the United States. But in 1824, when Josefina was a girl, it belonged to Mexico, and before that to Spain. In fact, Spain once ruled huge areas that are now part of the United States. Spanish and Mexican settlers first arrived in New Mexico more than 400 years ago, in 1598—even before the Pilgrims landed in America.

New Mexican settlers built homes in the mountains and valleys along the Rio Grande river. Santa Fe was the capital, but most settlers lived in villages and on ranchos. Drought was a constant worry, and so were sudden floods caused by heavy rainstorms. Lightning, grizzly bears, mountain lions, and rattlesnakes killed farm animals and sometimes people. To survive, everyone worked hard.

The settlers spoke Spanish, kept their Catholic faith, and enjoyed music and dances from Spain and Mexico. They grew familiar crops such as wheat, onions, and apples. They built irrigation ditches called *acequias* much like the ones used in Spain. But they also learned from their Pueblo Indian neighbors to use native foods like corn, squash, and pine nuts, and to make clothing such as moccasins.

Only a few villages had schools, but whether or not children learned to read and write, they received many kinds of education as they grew up. From their mothers, aunts, and grandmothers, girls learned the skills they needed to run a home of their own. A nine-year-old like Josefina would already know a great deal about sewing, knitting, spinning, weaving, cooking, gardening, and preserving food for the winter.

When winter came to the mountains of New Mexico, everyone began to look forward to Christmas, or *Navidad*. The Christmas season lasted nearly a month. It was a time for people to celebrate their faith and to enjoy evenings filled with delicious food, music, dancing, and the company of friends and relatives.

The *Camino Real*, or Royal Road, was the trail that connected Santa Fe with towns and cities hundreds of miles south. There, New Mexican goods such as wool blankets, animal hides, and pine nuts were traded for needed items like iron tools and luxuries like chocolate, Chinese silks and spices, and European lace, fabrics, and fine jewelry.

A caravan like Abuelito's took four or five months to reach Mexico City. There were deserts, canyons, mountains, and rivers to cross, and there was always the danger of attack. For more than 200 years the Camino Real was New Mexico's only link to the rest of the world. Then, in 1821, American traders began leading wagon trains from the state of Missouri to New Mexico. They made an important new trade route, which became known as the Santa Fe Trail. For the first time, people and goods from the United States began flowing into New Mexico.

Josefina's world was about to change.

GLOSSARY of Spanish Words

Abuelito *(ah-bweh-LEE-toh)*—Grandpa

acequia *(ah-SEH-kee-ah)*—a ditch made to carry water to a farmer's fields

adiós *(ah-dee-OHS)*—good-bye

adobe *(ah-DOH-beh)*—a building material made of earth mixed with straw and water

americano *(ah-meh-ree-KAH-no)*—a man from the United States

arroyo *(ah-RO-yo)*—a gully or dry riverbed with steep sides

bizcochito *(bees-ko-CHEE-toh)*—a kind of sugar cookie flavored with anise

buenos días *(BWEH-nohs DEE-ahs)*—good morning

Camino Real *(kah-MEE-no rey-AHL)*—the main road or trail that ran from Mexico City to New Mexico. Its name means "Royal Road."

colcha *(KOHL-chah)*—a kind of embroidery made with long, flat stitches

fandango *(fahn-DAHNG-go)*—a big celebration or party that includes a lively dance

feliz Navidad *(feh-LEES nah-vee-DAHD)*—Merry Christmas

gracias *(GRAH-see-ahs)*—thank you

gran sala *(grahn SAH-lah)*—the biggest room in the house, used for special events and formal occasions

granero *(grah-NEH-ro)*—a room used for storing grain, such as wheat and corn

la Noche buena *(lah NO-cheh BWEH-nah)*—Christmas Eve.

Las Posadas *(lahs po-SAH-dahs)*—a religious drama that acts out the story of the first Christmas Eve. Its name means "The Inns."

malacate *(mah-lah-KAH-teh)*—a long, thin spindle used to spin wool into yarn. New Mexicans used malacates instead of spinning wheels.

mano *(MAH-no)*—a stone that is held in the hand and used to grind corn. Dried corn is put on a large flat stone called a *metate*, and then the mano is rubbed back and forth over the corn to break it down into flour.

mantilla *(mahn-TEE-yah)*—a lacy scarf that girls and women wear over their head and shoulders

mayordomo *(mah-yor-DOH-mo)*—a man who is elected to take charge of town or church affairs

metate *(meh-TAH-teh)*—a large flat stone used with a *mano* to grind corn

Navidad *(nah-vee-DAHD)*—Christmas

Padre *(PAH-dreh)*—the title for a priest. It means "Father."

patrón *(pah-TROHN)*—a man who has earned respect because he owns land and manages it well, and is a good leader of his family and his workers

patrona *(pah-TROH-nah)*—a woman who has the responsibilities of a *patrón*

piñón *(pee-NYOHN)*—a kind of short, scrubby pine that produces delicious nuts

plaza *(PLAH-sah)*—an open square in a village or town

pueblo *(PWEH-blo)*—a village of Pueblo Indians

ramillete *(rah-mee-YEH-teh)*—a branch or bouquet of flowers used for decoration

rancho *(RAHN-cho)*—a farm or ranch where crops are grown and animals are raised

rebozo *(reh-BO-so)*—a long shawl worn by girls and women

sala *(SAH-lah)*—a room in a house

Santa Fe *(SAHN-tah FEH)*—the capital city of New Mexico. Its name means "Holy Faith."

sarape *(sah-RAH-peh)*—a warm blanket that is wrapped around the shoulders or worn as a poncho

Señor *(seh-NYOR)*—Mr.

Señora *(seh-NYO-rah)*—Mrs.

sí *(SEE)*—yes

siesta *(see-ES-tah)*—a rest or nap taken in the afternoon

tía *(TEE-ah)*—aunt

tortilla *(tor-TEE-yah)*—a kind of flat, round bread made of corn or wheat

Read more of JOSEFINA'S stories,

available from booksellers and at *americangirl.com*

⚜ *Classics* ⚜

Josefina's classic series, now in two volumes:

Volume 1:
Sunlight and Shadows

Josefina and her sisters are
excited when Tía Dolores
comes to their *rancho*, bringing
new ideas, new fashions, and
new challenges. Can Josefina
open her heart to change
and still hold on to precious
memories of Mamá?

Volume 2:
Second Chances

Josefina makes a wonderful
discovery: She has a gift for
healing. Can she find the
courage and creativity to mend
her family's broken trust in an
americano trader and to keep her
family whole and happy when
Tía Dolores plans to leave?

⚜ *Mystery* ⚜
A thrilling adventure with Josefina!

Secrets in the Hills

Josefina has heard tales of treasure buried in the hills, and of
a ghostly Weeping Woman who roams at night. But she never
imagined the stories might be true—until a mysterious stranger
arrives at her rancho.

A Sneak Peek at

Second Chances

A Josefina Classic
Volume 2

Josefina's adventures continue in the
second volume of her classic stories.

osefina opened one sleepy eye. Could she be dreaming? It was not quite dawn, and yet she seemed to hear music. Suddenly, Josefina grinned to herself. She remembered what day it was: the feast day of San José and her birthday.

Very slowly, the door to her room opened. In the pearly morning light she saw Papá, Tía Dolores, Ana and her husband Tomás, Francisca, Clara, Carmen the cook, and her husband Miguel. They began to sing:

> *On the day you were born*
> *All the beautiful flowers were born,*
> *The sun and moon were born,*
> *And all the stars.*

In the middle of the song, the little goat Sombrita poked her head around the corner of the door and bleated as if she were singing, too. Everyone laughed, and Tía Dolores said, "We wanted to surprise you with a lovely morning song, but I think someone forgot the words!"

Josefina picked up Sombrita and gave her a hug.

"Gracias," she said to everyone, feeling a little shy at all the attention. "I liked it."

The morning song was only the first surprise in a day full of them. Ana made cookies called *bizcochitos* for everyone to eat before breakfast. At morning prayers, Francisca showed Josefina how she'd decorated the family altar with garlands of mint and willow leaves and how she'd surrounded the statue of San José, the saint Josefina was named for, with white wild lilies and little yellow celery flowers. Clara, who liked to be practical, surprised Josefina by helping with her chores.

But when it was time to dress for the party, Clara had an impractical surprise for Josefina. It was a dainty pair of turquoise blue slippers. "It's about time I handed these down to you," said Clara. "I hardly ever wear them."

"Oh, Clara!" said Josefina, very pleased. She put the slippers on. They were only a *little* too big for her.

"If you're going to be so elegant," said Francisca, "you'd better carry Mamá's fan."

"And wear Mamá's shawl!" said Ana.

The four sisters shared Mamá's fan and shawl

and brought them out only on very special occasions. Josefina swirled the shawl around her shoulders and looked behind her to see the brilliant embroidered flowers and the slippery, shimmery fringe on the back. She fluttered the fan and felt very elegant indeed.

The party table looked elegant, too. There was a beautiful cloth on it, and the family's best plates and glasses and silverware. Tía Dolores had made a special fancy loaf of bread. There were meat turnovers, and fruit tarts, and candied fruit that looked like jewels. But best of all, in the center of the table there was a red jar with one small branch of apricot blossoms in it. Josefina smiled when she saw the perfect blossoms. She knew that Tía Dolores had cut the branch from *her* tree—the tree she liked to climb. Josefina remembered the day Tía Dolores had comforted her next to that apricot tree. "We're all given second chances," Tía Dolores had said. "We just have to be brave enough to take them."

About the Author

VALERIE TRIPP says that she became a writer because of the kind of person she is. She says she's curious, and writing requires you to be interested in everything. Talking is her favorite sport, and writing is a way of talking on paper. She's a daydreamer, which helps her come up with her ideas. And she loves words. She even loves the struggle to come up with just the right words as she writes and rewrites. Ms. Tripp lives in Maryland with her husband.